Matchmaking, Mistletoe and a Moat

by

Kim Janine Ligon

Christmas in the Castle Series

Publishing History
First Edition, 2024
Trade Paperback ISBN 978-1-5092-5854-3
Digital ISBN 978-1-5092-5855-0

Christmas in the Castle Series
Published in the United States of America

Dedication

Thank you Jim for your continued loving encouragement.

Thank you Millie and Beverly for being early readers and editors. I always appreciate your input.

Special thanks to Katie for reading and editing my early draft and especially for using your expertise on the Regency historical period to correct etiquette issues and for investing so much time to make the story shine. Couldn't have done it without you!

Thank you to my marvelous editor, Dianne Rich, for being willing to support my efforts in a whole new genre.

Thank you to my readers. I hope you enjoy this something a little different.

Thank you to the Lord who gives me stories to tell. I am truly blessed!

Chapter One

The clattering hoof beats slowed as the coach approached its destination, the Castle Winterhaven. The broad, wooden drawbridge spanning the dark waters of the moat groaned from the weight rolling over it. The cobblestone-paved path through the bailey hummed as the coach rolled forward. The four coal-black matched horses slowed. One of the lead horses whinnied.

The trip was longer than he had remembered. The Duke of Wallingford last visited Winterhaven nearly six years ago. A family gathering to celebrate the birth of his first nephew. He'd had pleasant company on that trip—his parents and older brother, Thomas—then he was merely Lord Greyford Parker, an inconsequential second son along for the ride to see the new addition to the family. Time and miles flew by with good conversation peppered with laughter and shared memories. Now he was a lone traveler with only his dread of the next two weeks to keep him company. A far cry from the last jolly expedition to the northern high country where his much loved sister lived.

The coach halted. Moments later the footman leapt down from his bench behind the vehicle, put the step stool in place, and opened the dust and mud caked door. The passenger put on his black silk top hat, ducked his head, and stepped out of the coach. He brushed the sleeves of his dust-covered dark coat and stomped the boots trying to loosen the travel dirt. He was glad to finally be able to stretch his six-foot two frame into a full standing position. Even riding alone had been cramped and mostly uncomfortable for the past three days. He swore this coach was made to accommodate his petite mother and sister, not the much larger men of his family.

A beautiful, raven-haired woman trailed by two small boys hurried out of the keep with her arms wide open. "Oh, Grey, you are finally here. I have been so anxious for you to arrive." She stood on tiptoe, pulled him down into an embrace, and kissed his cheek.

"You look marvelous, Caro. Marriage definitely agrees with you. Who are your shadows?" He kissed his twin sister's cheek and squatted to be at eye level with the small boys.

She hesitated a moment. "I have not heard that name in far too long. No one calls me Caro, but you. You remember Oliver. You came to visit soon after he was born. The younger one by a year who you have not met is Stephen. Boys, say hello to your distinguished uncle, Greyford Parker, the Duke of Wallingford."

The boys bowed politely from the waist. Oliver said, "It is a pleasure to meet you, Your Grace."

Grey embraced them. "Please call me Uncle Grey."

Oliver's face broke into a smile mirrored by Stephen's. "Yes, Uncle Grey," they said in unison.

Grey stood up with a nephew perched on each arm. "It is good I came to visit while they were still small enough for me to do this. They are quite an armload."

"It does my heart good to have you here for Christmas. It is especially comforting to be surrounded by your family's love and joy at this time of year.

Thank you for coming. Let us go in and get out of the cold." Caroline led the way into the entrance hall.

"Yes, it is good to see my charming sister and her family. I only wish the hospitable Countess Chelmsford and her distinguished husband had not planned their holiday house party to coincide with my visit. Sweet sister, I know what you are plotting and, for the record, I am not the least bit happy about it." He set the boys on their feet.

Caroline waved them away, "Go see if Cook has any special treats to tide you over until tea time." She turned to Grey and linked arms with him. "I know you are not pleased I have other guests, but it is past time you took action. Mama and Papa left us far too soon, shortly after your last visit here. Thomas has been gone a year last month. As the Duke of Wallingford you must select a mate and provide an heir. It is your duty. There will be a number of unattached, suitable, young women here over the holidays. Perhaps one of them will touch your bachelor's heart and inspire you to bring in the new year as a husband. It is my fondest wish."

"I know my responsibilities. You need not remind me. I frequently curse Thomas for not executing his. If he had married immediately six years ago instead of dissipating our family fortunes on fermented grapes and women of questionable morals, he would not have died in a drunken accident and foisted this unwanted, unexpected burden on me.

"I hope by 'suitable' you mean women of great beauty whose generous fathers are providing a more than usual dowry for their daughters. The estate has turned around in the past year, but without a substantial infusion of funds I shall not be able to keep it going. There are so many families who call Wallingford home and have served our family honorably for generations. I have to do this for them more than for myself." Grey's coal-black eyes flashed angrily for a moment.

"I know this is a major load for a second son who never expected to bear it. I hope you can relax and enjoy the season with us. Our other guests begin arriving tomorrow. Most will stay to see the new year enter here. It should be a conducive environment in which to get to know any potential duchess." Caroline patted his hand. "Let me show you to your room so you can get out of those dusty, wrinkled clothes before tea time. I believe your man should be there unpacking for you by now."

Jackson had not only unpacked, but managed to have a tub brought in and filled with perfect temperature bath water so the duke could scrub the three days' worth of travel grime off himself. A roaring fire kept the chill out of the room. Grey felt like a new man after the bath and clad in clean clothes.

He stepped to the window and opened it. What a glorious sight. The broad fells of the Pennine Chain Mountains abutted the outer ramparts of the castle. Just beyond the horizon lay Scotland. The air was crisp and clear. The blue sky was cloudless. Perhaps he would see snow on this visit. He shivered and pulled the window shut.

Jackson answered a knock at the door.

Oliver came in trailed by Stephen. "Excuse me, Uncle Grey. Mother says it is time for tea and thought you might need us to show you the way to the gold salon."

"Thank you. I was a little afraid I might get lost." He took a nephew by each hand and they went down the broad stone stairs into the entrance hall.

Tea was being served in the comfortable gold salon a short distance from there. Caroline had outdone herself decorating for the season. Fragrant pine boughs adorned each doorway and were draped across the fireplace mantel interspersed with mistletoe and holly with shining waxy berries amongst the greenery. Bright red ribbons and cinnamon-scented candles dotted the tables throughout the room lending a festive feel to the salon. A crackling fire in the massive fireplace made the room quite cozy and inviting.

The tall, curly-headed Earl of Chelmsford crossed the room with his hand extended. "Grey, it is so good to see you. I cannot tell you how excited and anxious your sister has been anticipating your arrival. I trust the travel was not too much of a strain." The men shook hands.

"Richard, good to see you as well. The trip was long but completely uneventful. Truth be told, I took the opportunity of the quiet coach ride to catch up on some much-needed sleep. I doubt your wife will leave me much time to rest while I am here." Grey winked at his blushing twin.

Caroline patted the sofa next to her. "Please sit beside me so we can talk. The boys just announced they are going to serve tea so I can have a rest. They learned the proper etiquette just for this occasion."

"What a surprise," Richard said laughing. "I had no idea our little hooligans could be so thoughtful."

"Father," Oliver said solemnly, "Nanny has been helping us plan this for over a week as a surprise.

Mother, how do you take your tea?"

"A spot of cream and a dash of honey, please."

Stephen said, "I know father only likes lemon." He handed his father's tea, with a slice of lemon balanced on the lip of the cup over to him.

"Uncle Grey, what will you have?"

"Please make mine exactly like your mother's."

Until the first scone found his mouth, Grey hadn't realized how hungry he was. It had been a long time since breakfast. He hadn't wanted to stop at midday for longer than it took to change horses. He was more eager to see his family than he wanted his sibling to know. So much had happened since his last visit.

His nephews very politely answered all Grey's questions and volunteered to take him to the stables in the morning to see the new foal that had been born yesterday. They had the honor of naming her but hadn't agreed yet on what the name would be. They asked if Uncle Grey would help them decide between Snow Beauty and Winter Wonder. He wanted to see the animal before he weighed in on the best choice.

When tea was over, Nanny came for her charges to return them to the nursery where they would stay the remainder of the evening. They shook hands with Uncle Grey and their father and enthusiastically hugged their mother before retreating upstairs. Caroline thanked Nanny for her part in the tea time surprise. The young woman blushed and nodded before herding the boys upstairs.

"Your sons are growing up so quickly," Grey observed.

"Yes, I told Caroline only yesterday we would need to find a governess or tutor soon to begin their education," Richard said.

"But they are only babies."

"Caro, we had a governess when we turned six. They have a lot to learn. I know you want them to stay little as long as possible, but I think Richard is right. How will they get into Eton if they are not properly educated at home?"

"Thank you, Grey, my point exactly."

"I do not like this development. I did not invite you here to side with my normally darling husband. Blood is supposed to be the stronger bond here. Richard is only related to you by marriage," Caroline protested.

"You are wrong, sweet sister. He is also kin to me by being a man," Grey said with a wink.

"You are both incorrigible. I shall leave you to your male bonding. I need to check on dinner." Caroline left the room.

Greyford had never spent much time with his brother-in-law. Caroline had her season and Richard whisked her away to the north in short order. He liked what he had seen of the earl and, clearly, the man adored his sister and their children. After seven years of marriage, he still seemed quite smitten with his wife.

"I hope you will forgive Caroline for inviting you here under the pretense of a family Christmas, then springing the holiday house party on you," Richard began.

Grey laughed. "I suspected there was a matrimony plot in the mix somewhere in the invitation. Caroline's letters are full of tidbits about the wonderful state of being married and having children. She thought I should be settling down long before Thomas's death. Now she believes it is imperative. And the sooner the better. I am certain she saw this as an opportunity to encourage me in the right direction. As you know, my sister can be almost impossible to satisfy until she gets her way. Were you driven to marry because you needed an heir?"

Richard smiled. "It is true my father had recently died when I met Caroline. But I married her because your sister completely bewitched me. I only attended the soirees of that season as a favor to my best friend who did not really want to be there but was in dire need of a wife. He met Caroline first, then introduced her to me and the rest you know. She was unlike any other woman I had ever met. Intelligent. Beautiful. Educated. She was interested in much more than balls and gowns. She asked lots of questions about Winterhaven and about living so close to Scotland. She was eager to know me, not just the man who could give her a title."

"I hope she will not be too disappointed when I leave in the new year without my own enchantress. I know it seems a little addled given my situation, but I want to actually love my wife. Forever. I have no need for a broodmare or the guarantee of an heir. I wish I could say a large dowry is not necessary. I need someone who is to me what Caroline is to you. A soul mate and the love of my life. Go ahead. Tell me I am an idiot to think I can find all that and the money too."

"My dear brother-in-law, I am the last person on earth who would tell you to settle for less than a perfect fit. I know how good it can be when it is right. Everyone should have this life."

Chapter Two

"Please, Papa, do not make me go on this husband hunt. I do not need to be married nor do I want to leave you. Please. Let me stay here and live out my days as a perfectly contented spinster caring for the father she adores." The tall chestnut-haired young woman stood with her hands clasped together prayerfully pleading with the gray-haired man behind the massive, polished desk. He removed his spectacles and rubbed his eyes.

"Emmeline Cordelia Spenser, how is it possible for you to grow more stubborn every single day?" The Earl of Crestmont looked skyward. "Amelia, I cannot believe you left me to deal with such a willful child alone. She certainly got your stubborn streak. Emmie, your aunt, Clementine, went to a great deal of trouble to get you invited to her dear friend's house party over the holidays. If you were to find a young man you wished to marry while you were there, it would be the answer to my fervent and frequent prayers."

"Papa, do you not want me to stay with you?" Emmeline batted back crocodile tears.

"I will not live forever and I cannot stand to think of you being ousted from your home. You know as well as I do you cannot stay here after my death unless you marry my cousin who inherits Crestwood and my title."

"Why can a woman rule Great Britain and I cannot inherit my family estate? It is simply not fair."

"I do not make the rules, my pet, but even our beloved sovereign, Queen Victoria, had to marry."

"At least she got to select her mate and she loves him. I am not marrying your third cousin, Hubert. I am only nineteen. He is older than you are. And his breath always reeks of garlic. I would join a convent before I would marry him. How could you wish that on me? Your only daughter?"

"I have no desire for you to marry Hubert or to take up the veil, but you missed your season when your mother died. Your friends are long-married and mothers to boot. It has been three years. My sweet Amelia would have wanted you to marry and give her grandchildren, give us grandchildren. Clementine has found an alternative which means you do not have to go through an entire season on what you so sarcastically describe as a husband hunt. It is only two weeks. Clementine and I will come to Winterhaven before the time is over. Please, would you go for my sake, so your aunt is not embarrassed by your rude refusal?"

"Yes, Papa, I will go to Winterhaven for the husband-hunting holiday party—on one condition."

"What is the condition?"

"Ellie comes with me. Then I would know someone other than my maid. Ellie could use a husband too. We are the same age. She did not have a season either since Mama planned we would have ours the same year."

"I agree to the condition. Your aunt actually garnered two invitations for the celebration. I talked with you first because I knew Eleanor would agree to whatever you did. You are right, perhaps Ellie will find a mate as well." He stepped to her side and pulled her into an embrace. "You and Ellie have been linked at the hip since you were both five years old. You might as well search for a spouse together. I am certain your mother and her sister, Cordelia, are smiling down on us seeing their daughters mirror their lives. They were as inseparable as you two are."

"Papa, who shall be our chaperone if you and Auntie are not coming until later?"

"Lady Agatha Crowley, a friend of your aunt's who happens to be the older sister of the Dowager Countess of Chelmsford. Her husband cannot travel over the holidays and she has not seen her sister in quite some time. It is working out perfectly."

Emmeline kissed her father's cheek and ran to find her cousin to tell her the news.

****

"Emmie, I will be totally out of place at Winterhaven," Eleanor protested. "I have no large dowry or family connections to offer a gentleman. I am only the orphan of a poor country vicar and his wife, who happened to be your mother's sister, and I had the good fortune to be raised at your side as if I would be a fine titled lady one day."

"Our mothers had their seasons together and found the loves of their lives. Remember, they had a double wedding. If I must do this, I can only bear it if you are with me. You will do fine with the crowd at Winterhaven. You speak four languages, are well-read, have a wicked sense of humor, can ride and hunt, and are incredibly beautiful!" Emmie laughed.

"You only think so because I look and behave exactly like you!" Ellie hugged her cousin. "I guess I can delay looking for a position until we return."

"A position? Where? Doing what?"

"It is time I stopped being a burden to your father. Especially if you leave to wed. I am perfectly educated to be a governess to some wealthy family. I love children so it would not be a hardship. If I never have the chance to birth my own, at least I can love someone else's. I shall postpone my position hunt until we return."

"We can discuss your plans when we return. Who knows, you may find someone who sweeps you off in a romantic storm of passion and carries you away to his castle somewhere. Then I shall be coming to live with you. Your poor little rich girl cousin."

Peals of laughter rang from them both. By dinner that evening they had finally chosen their wardrobes and warned their maid, Maisie, she would be accompanying them to a house party almost all the way to Scotland.

****

The coach ride began as a great adventure. They had never traveled so far from home without Papa, Mama, or Aunt Clementine to accompany them. Lady Crowley was a pleasant conversationalist and eager to tell the cousins all about Winterhaven. She had visited there many times before her brother-in-law died.

The weather was mild so Maisie rode atop the coach with the driver whom the cousins believed she was sweet on. Every bump in the road was a new and wonderful experience. The cousins chattered non-stop about the countess's house party, the scenery, and the special wonder of the Christmas season. Emmeline's mother always reveled in Christmas preparations. The bigger the celebration, the better. She was especially missed at this time of year.

They were exhausted by the time they reached the inn at Bell's Crossing on the first night. After a light supper of lentil soup and chicken, they both were sound asleep before Maisie turned out the lamp.

The second day they grew tired of the increasingly bumpy road nearly jarring them out of their seats and the unceasing dust that invaded the coach even with the blinds closed. It had driven Maisie away from her sweetheart and into the coach with them. Several times they drifted to sleep and woke due to Lady Crowley's snoring only to be disappointed they hadn't reached Winterhaven yet. One could look at just so much scenery before it all began to look the same.

They finally arrived at Winterhaven shortly after tea time and before dinner. The impressive castle glowed in the setting sun. The ramparts ran out to meet the foothills in the distance. The dark waters of the moat rippled as they crossed the drawbridge into the bailey. Their coach followed the cobblestone path to the front door of the keep. They were thankful to leave the constant motion of the coach after bouncing around for the better part of two days.

Lady Crowley remained in the coach and traveled on to the dower house to stay with her sister.

The cousins pled exhaustion to their hostess, Lady Chelmsford, who greeted them at the door and guided them to their room at the top of the broad stone stairs. A tub was sent to their sitting room and both of them enjoyed a bath in front of the roaring fire before they prepared for bed. The countess sent up two trays with a light fare so they could have a little something before retiring for the evening. They were hungry but mostly exhausted.

The next morning, Emmeline woke first. She quietly slipped out of bed, pulled on her warm, fluffy dressing gown, and stretched. She walked to the window and cracked it open. The glorious reds, oranges, and yellows of the rising sun painted the sky to her right. Directly ahead of her were the rising lands of the Pennines marching toward Scotland in the hazy distance. She closed the window, a little chilled, and stepped closer to the roaring sitting room fire.

She'd been too exhausted to appreciate their accommodations last evening. The holiday-decorated massive stone fireplace kept the sitting room and adjoining bedroom at a comfortable temperature. Pine boughs and holly formed a fragrant wreath above the fireplace, permeating the room with the fresh winter scent. More pine branches draped elegantly across the mantel below the wreath. The ornately carved chair in front of the fire dwarfed Emmie when she curled up in it to wait for Ellie to awaken. A shaggy black bearskin rug lay on the dark gray stone floor in front of the hearth.

Their massive bed with elaborately carved posts and headboard was more than ample for the cousins to share. Maisie was only a bell pull away in the servant's quarters. Emmie watched the crackling red and yellow flames dance across the giant logs in the fireplace and enjoyed the pleasant scent of pine wood smoke.

"How long have you been up?" Ellie came over and squeezed in the chair next to her cousin, wrapping a warm woolen blanket around them both.

"Not long. I did get out of bed in time to see the sun rise over the hills. It was breathtaking. I am afraid even after the restful night I am not ready for the party to begin today."

"Emmie, what are you worried about? Can you not relax? Just enjoy being somewhere we have never been before and meeting mysterious strangers. Would it be so horrible to find a husband while we are here? The worst part about the visit was the interminable coach ride. But we do not have to do that again for two weeks."

"Oh, Ellie, I did not tell Papa the truth. I do want to have a husband, but not a plain run-of-the-mill one. If I cared not what kind of man I marry, I could wait for old cousin Hubert to pop the question. I believe if I am not married by the time Papa is gone, he would feel compelled to propose. I need so much more than a mere man to be my husband. I want someone who sweeps me off my feet with passion. One who believes he cannot live without me—only me—in his arms forever. I need someone who will love me despite the size of my dowry, not because of it. I do not care if he is poor as a church mouse. If he makes my insides quiver when he kisses me and can make me weak in the knees with only a look then he is the one, the man I am destined to marry."

"My sweet cousin, you do not want much, do you? I think you have been reading too many novels. I am certain none of those men exist outside the pages of a book." Ellie laughed. "I guess it goes without saying he would be tall and handsome too."

"Maybe I got a little carried away. But I would take tall and handsome with the rest. I cannot figure out how I shall know for certain he is in love with me and not my generous dowry. I wish one of our mamas was here to talk to. I think they both found all that and more in our fathers. I do not know how they knew it was the right man to say yes to, but they did."

"Aunt Clementine would be more than happy to talk to us. She always seems to ask leading questions hoping we will ask for her advice. She thinks of us as her daughters now that we are both motherless. I think that is part of the reason she wrangled this invitation for us."

"I know, but her husband was so much older than she was and always so gruff. I do not think she had the same experience Mama did. I never saw him display any affection toward her. He was polite and seemed fond of her, but that is simply not enough for me. I cannot settle for polite companionship. I have noticed Auntie been in no hurry to marry again. She seems to be enjoying her widowhood. Uncle Charles has been gone five years. I want to be as happy as Mama always seemed. I want someone who will look at me like Papa gazed at her right until the end of her life. I knew they loved each other and loved me. He has been so lost without her."

"Emmie, I have an idea about how you could be certain you have found your true love—the one who loves you more than your dowry."

"How?"

"Be me."

"What are you talking about?"

"If someone falls in love with Eleanor Amelia Brown, orphan of a country vicar and his wife, then it must be genuine, forever, knee-weakening love. She has no dowry to entice him."

"Maybe…" Emmie broke into a grin. "You will be

me, Lady Emmeline Spenser, only child of the Earl of Crestmont, and I will be Miss Eleanor Brown. We have passed for twins in the past. Except for the three tiny moles on my left shoulder, we look exactly the same. We even have the same kind of lopsided smile. You would do this for me? What about finding true love yourself? I do not want to stand in your way."

Ellie laughed. "Maybe one of those dowry-seeking men will fall in love with me as Lady Emmeline and decide to marry me even after he discovers I have no money. That would have to be true love too. Let us get you married first, then we can worry about me. Remember, I have another plan to fall back on. I can be a governess. We had best ring for Maisie so we can get dressed and go to breakfast. I am rather hungry."

****

They walked into the bright and sunny breakfast room together. One wall of the room had French doors that opened onto a flagstone patio. A table to seat twelve was in the middle of the room with a holly branch and red candle centerpiece. A pastry laden buffet spanned one wall. It was a lovely, cheerful spot to have a little something to start the day.

Only two people were in the room—Lady Chelmsford and a handsome, raven-haired man at her side. They were in deep conversation at the far end of the table. The butler appeared and asked whether the cousins would like tea. They hesitated to sit near the countess, not wanting to interrupt her conversation.

Their hostess stood and invited them to the table. "Ladies, please come in. It is so good to see Lady Guilderwood's dear nieces, Lady Emmeline Spenser and Miss Eleanor Brown."

They walked to the end of the table where the countess was seated and curtsied in greeting. "Good morning, Lady Chelmsford. Guilty as charged. I apologize we were unable to join you for dinner last night. We were exhausted from the trip," Emmeline said.

"I understand completely. Let me look at you. Clementine told me you two could pass for twins. I thought that was a biased aunt's observation, but I have never seen two young women who looked so much alike but were not twins, not even sisters, but cousins." Lady Chelmsford leaned back and looked at the pair who both had chestnut hair styled alike, sparkling green eyes, and lush eyelashes. "How will we keep you straight?"

"We will try to help. We are accustomed to being mistaken for one another. Our mothers were identical twins. Aunt Clementine was their older sister. I am Miss Eleanor Brown, and she is Lady Emmeline Spenser," the real Emmeline said.

"It is a pleasure to meet you both. This is my brother, His Grace the Duke of Wallingford, Greyford Parker."

The duke stood and made a short bow to the ladies. "I am pleased to make your acquaintance, Lady Emmeline and Miss Eleanor."

"Your Grace, a pleasure to meet you." Eleanor said.

Emmeline said, "Your Grace, how nice to meet you."

"Lady Chelmsford, I will leave you to become better acquainted with your guests. I need to visit the hothouse and check on the surprise I brought you for

Christmas. Ladies, I hope you enjoy your breakfast."

"You are welcome to stay with us. I am sure we will not be discussing any women only topics," Caroline said laughing.

"I do not want to put a damper on your conversation." The duke bent and kissed his sister's cheek.

The butler appeared with their tea. "Lady Emmeline, Miss Brown, what will you have for breakfast?" The cousins ordered their meal and returned to the conversation with their hostess.

"I am so glad you could both join us for our Christmas into New Year's celebration. Lady Emmeline, I understand Clementine and your father will be joining us soon after Christmas."

"Yes, Lady Chelmsford," Emmeline answered and then realized who she was supposed to be. "My uncle, Emmeline's father, told us they planned to be here later in the celebration."

"I am glad you could both join us. I have an even number of men and ladies. It is not critical but it makes dining arrangements and dancing easier to pair people together. I hate for anyone to feel like an unwanted extra. Please call me Caroline."

"Thank you, Lady Caroline. I hope I am not being rude to comment, you said we look alike, but so do you and your brother," Eleanor said.

"We are twins."

"Are you the only children in your family?" Emmeline asked.

"We had an older brother, Thomas. He died over a year ago leaving the title and estate to His Grace. It is no secret he is a very eligible bachelor who needs to find a bride. I understand both of you ladies are also unattached and of a marriageable age."

Eleanor blushed. "Yes, Lady Caroline. You are correct."

"You will not be the only single women here. Last night, Lady Cecilia Thompson and her sister Lady Beatrice arrived from Cumbria. They are the daughters of the Earl and Countess of Glenwood. Viscount Ashleigh, William Benedict, and Viscount Summerly, Simon Hartsfield, joined us from nearby Northumberland. You are the early birds. None of them have appeared for breakfast yet. Today there are a dozen more guests arriving. I plan to have a light luncheon buffet set up for midday. I do not have anything formal planned until tea at five this afternoon.

"You are free to wander about the castle and grounds. Riding horses and buggies are available in the stable if the weather continues to improve. Please take the day and enjoy getting to know Winterhaven. The only word of warning is about the towers. Most of the castle has been extensively renovated over the past twenty years, except for the two towers. They are in their original condition. They can be tricky to negotiate especially if wind and rain are present. I recommend only visiting them with a member of my staff or family for added safety. They have wonderful views of the Pennines and the entire estate so we shall have to make certain you have an opportunity to visit them before you leave. I expect you will run into some of the other guests by afternoon. Now I must check on my children. Please excuse me."

After the countess left, Emmeline said, "You are going to have to speak more. People expect Lady

Emmeline to be the chatty one."

"I would be happy to, cousin, if Miss Brown will kindly be quiet long enough for me to do so." She winked at Emmeline. Breakfast arrived and was enjoyed by them both.

Chapter Three

The cousins decided to explore the castle first. Then when it warmed a little, the rest of the grounds. There were at least eight bedrooms on the first floor. Their room was easy to find since it was at the top of the broad stone stairs rising from the entrance hall. The floor above them mirrored theirs. The Earl and Countess of Chelmsford and their children had the entire top floor for their personal bed chambers, nursery, and solar. The cousins didn't go all the way upstairs to the private living area.

The Great Hall off the main entrance was filled with tables with pine bough and holly centerpieces running down the middle of them. The two massive stone fireplaces had festive greenery draped across their mantels. The air was filled with the pungent scents of cloves, cinnamon, and pine.

"I have not been looking forward to Christmas," Eleanor said. "But this room is whisking me into the magical feeling of the season."

"It is quite beautiful. I love the tapestries. I know they are not Christmas decorations but they are exquisite. What craftsmanship, the amazing weaving. They must tell stories of the castle's early times. Look at the battle swords raised and flashing shields. The war horses are magnificent creatures. Papa said this was one of the important fortresses for the king when the Scots rose up against the British crown in the past. We shall have to ask the earl about his family history. I wonder if his ancestors always had this castle."

"I love the way the renovations have been done to retain the feel of the original castle. It is a cozy family dwelling and a stalwart fortress all rolled into one," Eleanor said. "Let us get our cloaks and bonnets and explore outside."

"Can we walk to the base of one of the towers and peek in? I know we cannot really explore them without a guide, but I am intrigued," Emmie asked.

"All right, but only a glance. We do not want to be thought rude for going in the wrong place on our first full day here."

****

The sun shone brightly, warming the air to a slight briskness. They were quite comfortable in their bonnets and wool cloaks. The cousins strolled across the bailey to the base of a tower. An oversized wooden door at the bottom of the structure was partially ajar. The hinges groaned and squealed when the cousins worked together and shoved the massive door fully open. A musty smell assaulted their noses once they stood inside the tower at the bottom of the stairs which trailed upward beyond their line of sight.

"All right, Emmie. You have stuck your head in. May we leave now? This is a little spooky."

"I would love to climb those stairs. Imagine the view from the turret window."

"Imagine the cold wind! You promised we would only look today, not scale the stairs. Lady Caroline said she would make certain we got to visit before we leave."

"You win, Eleanor. I shall save the exploration for later when I'm bored with playing Whist and charades."

On the grassy bailey outside the keep, vendors were beginning to set up tents and tables in preparation for a carnival. The castle grounds would welcome not only the holiday house party goers, but the families from the nearby village and those of the castle workers for an early Christmas feast and celebration.

"How exciting! I feel like a little girl," Ellie said.

"The Rom are here. There is a gypsy vardo parked on the far side of the grass. Look at the intricate carving and the bold, bright colors painted on its side. Maybe they will have a fortune teller who can reveal to me who my true love will be to save me time finding him."

"You are incorrigible, Emmeline."

"Look, the stables are over to the right. Is it not the perfect day for a ride in the countryside?" Emmie asked.

"Lady Caroline said we could use the horses. Let us do so."

Halfway to the stables, they met the duke trailed by two small boys. He stopped in front of them and tipped his hat. "Good morning, ladies. Is it not a glorious day?"

"Yes, Your Grace, it seems perfect for a gambol down the trails. Have you been out riding?" Eleanor asked.

"No, my nephews and I have been naming the new foal in the stables. Let me present Lord Oliver Winter and the Honorable Stephen Winter." The boys bowed briefly. "These lovely ladies are Lady Emmeline Spenser and Miss Eleanor Brown."

"Excuse me, Uncle Grey. Which one is which?"

Oliver asked.

"I was afraid you would ask that question. I must confess, I cannot tell them apart. Ladies, would you mind?"

"Not at all. I am Miss Eleanor and this is my cousin, Lady Emmeline."

"Pleased to meet you," the boys said in unison.

'Lady Emmeline' stooped down to speak with them, "What did you name your new foal?"

"Uncle Grey picked a totally different name than the two choices we gave him," Stephen said.

"Do you like what he chose?" 'Miss Brown' asked.

"Yes, Miss Eleanor. The choices were Snow Beauty and Winter Wonder. You see, she is completely white," Oliver said.

"But Uncle Grey named her Winter Beauty," Stephen interrupted breathlessly.

"Sounds like your uncle is a diplomat," 'Miss Brown' said with a smile.

"Oh, no, Miss Eleanor. He is a duke," Oliver said seriously.

'Miss Brown' put a hand to her mouth trying to suppress a giggle.

"You are a duke, right, Uncle Grey?" Oliver asked.

"Yes. You are correct. Miss Eleanor was being clever." The duke looked at her with an arched eyebrow.

"So what is a diplomat?" Stephen asked.

"I will explain it on the way back to the keep. Come along, we have detained these ladies long enough." The duke took a nephew in each hand and bowed to the cousins. His eyes met 'Miss Brown's' and held her attention longer than was probably proper for people who'd only just met before he turned away. Her stomach did a flip flop and she swallowed hard. She was thankful he could no longer see her face which she was certain from the wave of heat across her cheeks was turning red.

"Now that is a handsome man. And he seems quite comfortable around children," 'Lady Emmeline' teased her cousin.

There were several other people wandering near the stables. Clearly, also guests for the holiday gathering. As the cousins approached them, a tall gentleman with sandy-colored hair and a matching van dyke beard tipped his hat and spoke, "Good morning, ladies. Do you have a gambol about the countryside in mind also?"

"Yes, we do," 'Miss Brown' replied.

He bowed slightly. "Forgive my forwardness. I am William Benedict, Viscount Ashleigh, and my companion is Simon Hartsfield, Viscount Summerly. We arrived early last evening."

"Gentlemen, I am Miss Eleanor Brown, and this is my cousin, Lady Emmeline Spenser."

'Lady Emmeline' nodded in her best imitation of nobility.

"Might I suggest we accompany you on your ride?" Lord Summerly asked. The auburn-haired gentleman had the bluest eyes Eleanor had ever seen. She knew she was blushing when he caught her staring at him.

"Thank you. You are most kind. We both are experienced riders, but you never know what may happen on a strange horse on an unfamiliar trail," 'Lady Emmeline' said with a smile.

The stablemaster assured the cousins their mounts were accustomed to lady riders and were extremely gentle beasts. He brought a step stool to the side of each horse to allow 'Miss Brown' and then 'Lady Emmeline' to mount the horse's side saddle. He recommended a trail which would return them to the castle in time for the midday luncheon.

Emmeline had intended for the cousins to follow behind the gentlemen so they could converse together. Lord Ashleigh had a different idea. He arranged to be at 'Miss Brown's' side while Lord Summerly rode abreast with 'Lady Emmeline'.

The trail was heavily wooded. The trees were leafless but beautiful. Pine trees dotted the landscape as well. The rocks from the Pennines lay in groups along the trail and it seemed as if you could see forever. Their conversations were mainly about the scenery, but quite pleasant.

The quartet returned to the stables in time to get back to the castle and freshened up before the luncheon which was served in the same room breakfast had been in. Lentil and sausage soup, finger sandwiches, and marvelous raspberry tarts were available. The perfect amount to whet one's appetite.

The cousins excused themselves after eating, retrieved the books they were reading from their room, donned their cloaks and bonnets, and returned to the garden to read in the comfortable bright sunshine. Nothing was flowering at this time of year but there was a pleasant bench to sit on in the middle of the garden near the goldfish pond. A generous splash of evergreen shrubbery brightened the area.

"Cousin, every time I look at you, you are not

reading. Where are you?" Ellie asked.

Emmie blushed. "I am afraid to say it out loud."

"There is no one here but us. Tell me."

The blush deepened to more red than pink. "I am wrapped in the Duke of Wallingford's arms. He is kissing me passionately and murmuring words of love in my ear. Are you aghast that I should be thinking of him in such a way when I only met him today?"

"No," Ellie said, "I must confess I have been melting into Lord Summerly's amazing blue eyes ever since meeting him this morning."

"My goodness, we have become brazen hussies. We had best subdue those lusty thoughts and get back to our reading. This is only the beginning of our two weeks here." Emmie laughed.

"And we have no idea if the gentlemen in question can even tell us apart!"

****

Seats in the salon were filling quickly when the cousins walked into the room at tea time. Lords Summerly and Ashleigh noticed 'Miss Brown' and 'Lady Spenser' immediately and made a beeline over to greet them.

The Duke of Wallingford stood in front of the fireplace smoking a pipe and talking to his brother-in-law. He nodded a greeting to the ladies. Emmeline was certain the innocent bob of his head immediately painted her cheeks pink. What a handsome man. And when he smiled in her direction, she swore she felt her knees grow weaker. How could he affect her that way? She'd barely met him. It was something about those coal-black eyes. They seemed to look into her soul.

Two women about the same age as Emmeline and

Eleanor crossed the salon to introduce themselves. Eleanor suspected the cousins weren't the people they wanted to meet but rather the women were interested in the handsome lords conversing with the cousins.

Lady Cecilia Thompson was a willowy blonde with a too ready raucous laugh and ever present smirk. Her sister, Lady Beatrice, was a much shorter and stouter woman with mousy brown hair with a shy smile. Much to Eleanor's dismay, Lady Cecilia gushed over everything Lord Summerly said and laughed—no— cackled—overly loudly at any of his attempts at humor. Lady Beatrice was charming and reserved, rarely raising her voice above a medium whisper. Lord Ashleigh hung on Lady Beatrice's every word, although Emmeline thought the woman was oblivious to the effect she had on the viscount.

The six new acquaintances conversed throughout tea time while enjoying tasty pastries and copious amounts of tea. Lord Summerly sat between Lady Cecilia and 'Lady Emmeline' on one settee while Lord Ashleigh sat between 'Miss Brown' and Lady Beatrice.

The duke sat on one side of his sister and her husband on the other. He commented, "My sweet sister is a rose between two thorns while the gentlemen across the room appear to be thorns growing among the roses."

Lady Cecilia's cackle pierced the air as it had frequently throughout the gathering. Emmeline shuddered each time the shrill nasal noise erupted.

Lady Chelmsford introduced a new arrival who appeared halfway through tea. "This is my brother-in-law, The Honorable Paul Winter." She crossed the room and kissed his cheek. The broad-shouldered man with blond-colored curly hair seemed slightly embarrassed by the attention his sister-in-law lavished upon him. He followed her to meet all of the assembled guests.

More guests were expected by dinner time: the Earl and Countess of Bollingwood and their daughter, Cornelia Peters; the Earl and Countess of Castleberry and their son, Edward Conrad; the Duke of Wingate; and the Dowager Countess Chelmsford and her sister, Lady Agatha Crowley. The complement of guests would not be complete until after Christmas when Lady Spenser's father, the Earl of Crestmont, and her aunt, Lady Clementine Guilderswood joined the party.

****

Shortly after the cousins finished dressing for dinner, a large gilded carriage clattered across the cobblestones and stopped in front of the keep. Emmeline and Eleanor observed the new arrivals from their bedroom window.

A short, and quite rotund man stepped out of the carriage. He held his hand out for an equally plump woman who must be his mate, and then a very slight young woman followed the woman who must be her mother from the coach.

Emmie leaned over and whispered, "It must be Earl and Countess of Bollingwood and their daughter, Cornelia. How did such a small girl come from those two?"

Ellie laughed. "I am afraid I shall not be able to look at them without thinking of Humpty Dumpty."

"I wish you had never said that. How shall I keep from giggling when we are around them?"

Immediately after the first coach emptied, another rolled across the groaning moat drawbridge. A very tall, thin man alit from the carriage followed by a tall, thin woman, and a young dark-haired man of average height but also on the lean side.

"They must be the Earl and Countess of Castleberry and their son Edward," Ellie said.

"Do not say what you are thinking. I cannot have another silly reference floating around in my brain. We need to join the party in the gold salon and meet all the new arrivals and forget the descriptive nursery rhymes."

Their hostess greeted them in the gold salon. She confirmed their suspicions. The rotund trio was the Peters family—Lord and Lady Bollingwood and daughter, Cornelia. And the long, thin trio were the Conrad family—Lord and Lady Castleberry and son, Edward. Emmeline and Eleanor managed to control their mirth and properly greet the newcomers.

There was a distinguished older gentleman in front of the fireplace in conversation with the duke. He was introduced as Wallingford's godfather and old family friend, His Grace, the Duke of Wingate, Jonathon Marley.

A regal woman with silver curls and a developing double chin was the Dowager Countess of Chelmsford, Lady Margaret Winter, Lord Richard and Paul's mother and Lady Chelmsford's mother-in-law. She resided in the dower house which was across the bailey from the keep. She introduced the woman seated next to her, their chaperone, Lady Agatha Crowley. The sisters looked very much alike right down to their chins.

At dinner, the cousins learned Lords Bollingwood and Castleberry, with the Duke of Wingate had all attended Eton with the father of Lord Chelmsford and Paul Winter. Their children had been raised together—

Richard, Paul, Edward, and Cornelia. They had spent many happy hours in one another's company at holiday gatherings over years past.

After dinner, the ladies paired up for Whist. 'Lady Emmeline' and 'Miss Eleanor' against Lady Cecilia and Lady Beatrice at one table. Lady Cornelia and Lady Bollingwood versus Lady Castleberry and Lady Margaret Chelmsford at another. Lady Caroline and Lady Crowley visited nearby. The gentlemen migrated to Lord Richard's library for brandies, cigars, and a heated political discussion.

Lady Cecilia berated her sister and partner throughout their play. 'Eleanor' was embarrassed for the mousy older sister. When Cecilia distractedly threw a trump card then led with the suit she had just trumped, Beatrice pointed out her faux pas. Cecelia snorted and swept the cards all onto the floor ending the match.

"It is a foolish game. I would much rather be having brandy and a good cigar in the library with the gentlemen." She stormed out of the salon.

"I apologize for my sister," Beatrice began. "I am sure she would have preferred the company of the gentlemen. She is not usually so difficult to get along with. Traveling is stressful for her and she is trying hard to make a good impression with the duke. She is positive nothing will do except that she will be the next Duchess of Wallingford. Oh, I should not have shared that tidbit. Please do not say anything. She will have my head."

"Do not worry, your secret is safe with us." Lady Caroline patted her shoulder. "She definitely has her work cut out for her if she believes the Duke of Wallingford can be easily lured into matrimony by a pretty face. My brother is a man of strongly held opinions and desires. It will be interesting to see how this battle of wills comes out."

The gentlemen rejoined the ladies in the salon and everyone said their good nights.

****

Maisie turned out the lamp and retired to the servant's quarters.

The cousins nestled under the covers, but not to sleep. It had been a lovely, if a little tiring, day.

"I think we are the fresh marriage market meat along with Cecelia and Beatrice. At least, among the husband hunters. I guess Lords Ashleigh, Summerly, and Castleberry are some new husband material. Cornelia is well known to the duke and Paul Winter. She is quite beautiful with her jet-black hair and bright blue eyes. I am surprised one of them has not married her before now if they were so inclined," Emmie observed.

"Or that Cornelia and Edward have not tied the knot. Edward seemed to be deliberately ignoring Cornelia. He is handsome in a rugged sort of way. Maybe they are all too familiar with one another. Rather like marrying your brother instead of a lover who causes your knees to go weak and your heart to palpitate. Makes you wonder what the real story is behind all the hunters and the prey, does it not?" Ellie laughed.

"Did you meet anyone today to pull your attention away from the blue eyes of Lord Summerly?"

"No. Not that I was comparison shopping." She laughed again. "Is the duke the only who sets your heart a flutter?"

"I never said he did that!"

"Oh, did I mishear you earlier?"

"No. Why is it every time he even glances in my direction I am certain he knows exactly what I am thinking? He probably is not even looking at me. I get the feeling he is not very happy about being paraded around as husband material. He seems to think we are all silly schoolgirls. I hope he really is noticing me in a positive way. Oh, Ellie, why does everything have to be so dramatic and difficult?"

"I do not know, sweet cousin. We shall not solve the mysteries of life tonight. Tomorrow is another day. Have beautiful dreams. Good night."

Chapter Four

At breakfast the next morning, Lord Summerly invited 'Lady Emmeline' to go horseback riding again and Lord Ashleigh extended an invitation to Lady Beatrice. Lady Cornelia and The Honorable Paul Winter rounded out the party.

"Emmie, I hate to leave you alone here, but I could not say no when I looked into those amazing eyes."

"Do not be silly, Ellie. Have a wonderful time. We do not have to do everything together. I definitely have no desire to be the extra-what-do-we-do-with-her-female. I am quite capable of keeping myself entertained. It is a great opportunity for you to get better acquainted with Lord Summerly."

It was another sunny day with only a slight nip in the air. The party on horseback departed after promising to return in time for luncheon.

'Miss Brown' asked one of the servants where to find what she was looking for and set off.

****

After leaving the breakfast room the duke rounded the corner quickly and ran into Lady Cecelia. Her head to his chest. He grabbed her shoulders and waist to keep her from falling to the ground.

"Your Grace." The willowy blonde batted her eyes. "Please unhand me. What will people think? We've only recently met."

He quickly dropped his arms away from her side. "I was only trying to keep you upright, Lady Cecelia. No insult was intended. Forgive me. In my haste to get to the library, I failed to watch where I was going."

"Of course, you are forgiven, Your Grace. I would love to go to the library with you. Sounds like a perfect out of the way place where we could get to know one another better."

"It would be highly inappropriate for us to be without a chaperone—alone. Have you no regard for your reputation? I must insist you find amusements elsewhere, Lady Cecelia."

She continued to trail behind him. "But Your Grace, you do not know me. Not the real me. The one who would make a magnificent duchess standing by your side. Please, let us not be so formal. My friends call me CeCe. Can we not be friends? You were flirting with me at dinner last evening. Were you not? It is fine. I enjoyed it. Tremendously," she purred. She reached out and laid her hand on his forearm.

The duke turned at the library door and gently removed her hand from his arm. "Lady Cecelia, I know you well enough for my purposes. I merely conversed politely at dinner, extending to you the same common courtesy I have given to all of the guests in my sister's home. This is my destination. I would appreciate you giving me the privacy I have requested. I have some pressing business matters I need to research. I have no time for any company, yours or others. Please do not press me further or you will embarrass us both."

"Are you certain you do not want to change your mind, Your Grace? I can be very helpful in certain circumstances." She licked her lips.

She tried to follow him into the library. He firmly shoved her out of the doorway and closed the door before the stunned woman could react. He leaned against the door half expecting her to attempt to push her way in despite his very clear request that she not follow him.

"I do not know if I can ever forgive Caroline for putting me in the middle of these marriage-hungry harpies." He ran his fingers through his black curls in exasperation leaving them sticking out all over.

"Oh, no!" a clearly female voice rang out from above. Then two thuds echoed through the room. A volume of Plato's *Dialogues* and *Wuthering Heights* were lying on the carpet at Grey's feet.

"What in heaven's name?"

Greyford looked at the rolling ladder that extended to the top shelves of the library. A chestnut-haired young woman clung to a rung by one arm and had two more books in the other. She seemed suspended from the ceiling like a literary angel.

"Did you follow me too?" he bellowed angrily. "I cannot even escape to the library."

"Your Grace, clearly I was here well before you. Were you trailing after me?" She smiled in an exaggerated way.

"Come down from there this instance. I am getting a crick in my neck from having to turn awkwardly to speak to you up there."

"Your Grace, will you take these books so I can hold on with both hands, please?"

"Fine. Drop them to me one at a time." She carefully let each volume fall into his waiting hands. "Egad, woman, you are only here ten more days. When will you ever have time to finish all these tomes?"

"I read very quickly, Your Grace. Besides, I have no interest in the mating rituals in progress around me. I shall have plenty of time to read while my cousin is otherwise occupied."

"Which one of the cousins are you?"

"Your Grace, I am Miss Eleanor Brown. Does it matter?"

"No. Of course not. I was merely being polite to inquire whom I was in the company of. Please come down before I am permanently disfigured."

She carefully started down the ladder. Slowly. Holding on with both hands. One rung at a time. When the hem of her skirt was at the duke's shoulder level, she completely stopped.

"Oh, dear. My left foot will not move."

"Why not?"

"I believe one of the buttons on my shoe has caught on the rung somehow. I cannot get it free."

"May I be of assistance?"

"Your Grace, it would be highly inappropriate for you to touch any part of my person. Especially as we are alone."

"Would you prefer to remain suspended above my head until I can find one of the servants to help me? You appear to be listing somewhat precariously."

"I am afraid I am becoming quite dizzy from looking down. Please, help me. Now."

The duke looked at the problem from the side. "I see what is wrong. This one button is wedged between the rung and the small gap with the side of the ladder. I will have to grasp your foot at the heel and ankle to turn it enough to free the offending button. Are you ready for me to touch you?"

She stared into his coal-black eyes, took a deep breath, and nodded. The duke put both hands on her foot. His touch felt like fire burning through her shoe. He gently turned her foot while pulling it backward away from the ladder. "Voila! Miss Brown, you are free."

'Miss Brown' opened her eyes and looked around. She had been freed from the ladder's grasp and was on the ground. Oh, mercy. No. She was sitting atop the duke's chest and *he* was lying flat on the ground. His eyes were closed. She gently slapped his cheek to get his attention. "Your Grace, are you hurt?"

"I will be fine as soon as you get off of me," he growled through clenched teeth.

'Miss Brown' rolled off her rescuer. He stood and bent down to help her stand, but lost his balance and fell to the ground ending up sitting with her in his lap. There was nothing to do but laugh. And they both did. Loudly.

"Well, now I understand why you had no desire for me to join you in the library. Is this what you call business research, Your Grace?" Lady Cecelia stood a few feet from them with a hateful expression on her face and her hands firmly on her hips. "What unseemly behavior. You must be the poor country cousin. Lady Emmeline would know better than to behave like this. Did you think if you let him ruin your reputation he would be forced to make you his duchess?"

The duke pulled himself to his feet again and aided 'Miss Brown' to a standing position. "Lady Cecelia, you are quite mistaken. I understand the situation looks bad but I have done nothing untoward or inappropriate to ruin Miss Brown's reputation. I merely helped get her shoe's button unstuck from the library ladder so she could get to the ground."

"Your Grace, of all the ridiculous stories. You could not think of something more plausible? What makes you think this country bumpkin could make a duchess? Do you not know the old saying you cannot make a silk purse from a sow's ear? And I know a sow's ear when I see one even if you do not."

"Lady Cecelia, your comments are completely out of line." The duke stepped toward her.

"Please, Your Grace, you have no need to defend me or my honor from this doxy masquerading as a fine lady. I believe she doth protest too much. Tell me, Lady Cecelia, are you jealous you failed to think of this ruse first?"

Lady Cecelia stepped forward and slapped 'Miss Brown'. Hard. The lady pulled her arm back to do it again but the duke caught her hand and stopped it. "I will not be spoken to as if I were a commoner by the likes of her. Stay out of my way, Eleanor Brown, or you will rue the day if we ever meet alone." She pulled out of the duke's grasp and stormed out of the room, slamming the door as she left.

Grey put his hand under 'Miss Brown's' chin and tipped her head. He could clearly see the reddening outline of Lady Cecelia's angry handprint. "Are you going to be all right?"

"I shall be fine, Your Grace. Thank you for rescuing me from the ladder and from Lady Cecelia's second slap. I am not surprised she hit me. She has shown quite a temper before but this totally was my fault. I should resist always saying what I am thinking.

Papa had warned me frequently about being too sassy. Her obsessive desire to wed you is none of my business. If you will hand me the books, I shall be on my way. I think a cool cloth will remove the redness from my cheek before anyone else sees it."

He gathered the books and loaded them into her waiting arms. "Are you certain I cannot carry them to your sitting room for you?"

"I have caused enough trouble for you today. We cannot risk being caught without a chaperone again. Thank you, Your Grace."

Grey opened the library door for 'Miss Brown'. What did she mean about Lady Cecelia trapping him into a proposal? He would have to talk to Caro. He had no idea looking for a wife could be so dramatic or that the ladies would play the game like a bunch of cut-throats.

****

The horseback riders came into the luncheon laughing, all talking simultaneously. Even shy Lady Beatrice was smiling and animated. She and Lord Ashleigh seemed well suited to one another. Lord Summerly did not let 'Lady Emmeline' get out of his reach, making certain she sat next to him at the table. Paul Winter and Lady Cornelia were having a friendly conversation peppered with laughter and teasing like the old friends they were.

"It sounds like the horseback riding was a great success this morning," Lady Caroline said.

"It was a perfect day for the ride," Paul Winter said.

"Glorious sunshine," Lady Beatrice added.

"And outstanding companions," Lord Summerly

chimed in.

Grey entered the room and stopped to kiss his sister's cheek. He quickly scanned the faces searching for 'Miss Brown'. Had she recovered from the morning's trauma?

"I am afraid Lady Cecelia is lying down. She is getting a sick headache and begs not to be bothered. She took some medication and is going to try to sleep it off so she can join the evening's festivities," Lady Caroline said. She had immediately gone to speak with her guest after her brother reported the misunderstanding from the library meeting.

"I hope she is able to recover quickly," 'Miss Brown' said as she entered the room.

Grey was relieved no trace of the handprint lingered on her face. She appeared fully recovered. He hadn't appreciated before how hauntingly beautiful her emerald-green shining eyes were. Why had he noticed them now? Miss Eleanor Brown certainly wasn't the answer to his financial woes. Her cousin perhaps, they did have the same green eyes. Yet, something about them was distinctly different. Besides, Lady Emmeline Spenser was being closely attended by Lord Summerly. Why should it matter to Grey who was courting anyone? Caroline and her marriage fever. His sister was an infectious, unstoppable force when she got a notion.

Chapter Five

Emmeline and Eleanor retired to their rooms for a brief rest after lunch. As soon as the door was closed behind Maisie, they began talking at the same time.

Emmeline laughed. "Sounds like we have both had an eventful morning. You go first. Lord Summerly seems to be quite smitten by you, Lady Emmeline."

"Is Simon not marvelous?" Ellie gushed.

"Simon is it now. Things have progressed far in a short period of time."

"I guess they have." Ellie's cheeks reddened. "Simon said he only came to Winterhaven as a favor to Lord Ashleigh, his best friend. William, Lord Ashleigh, needs to find a wife. He stands to inherit a title and quite a lot of wealth when his uncle dies, but a new will says William can only do so if he is married before he turns twenty-one. His twenty-first birthday is at the end of January. He and Lady Beatrice are getting along famously."

"Good news for Lord William and Lady Beatrice. What is Simon's status?"

"Simon is an only child and his position as the Earl of Summerton is assured at the death of his father. He said he was not in a rush to marry—until he met me. Now he wants to know if I could be happy with him."

"Oh, Ellie, how wonderful. Then your dowry situation will not matter a lick to him.

"I think you are right, but I feel guilty for deceiving him. He may be unconcerned about my lack of money, but do you think he will feel the same when he discovers I am Miss Brown and not Lady Emmeline?"

"I do not know, but I have to ask you to playact a little longer. We only got here a few days ago and my prospects are not as promising as yours, not yet."

"What happened this morning?"

"Shortly, after you left to go riding, I located the library. I decided to catch up on my reading and Lady Chelmsford told me I was welcome to borrow whatever books struck my fancy."

"How is hiding in the library going to find you a match, Emmie?"

"I am getting to that. I was up near the top of the ladder selecting books when I heard someone come in the room. I froze. It was the duke and he was not alone. He was being pursued by Lady Cecelia. She was quite insistent that he let her come in the library with him. He finally escaped her clutches, closed the library door, made some comments about husband-hunting harpies, and then I dropped two books right at his feet making a terrific racket. He seemed furious that he wasn't alone and more angry when he realized who had made the noise. He demanded that I come down to the ground immediately. I handed him the books I had selected that I still had in my hand. I started down the ladder and the button on my left shoe got caught between the ladder side and a rung. I could not go up or down. I was stuck above his head."

"What did you do?"

"I told the duke I was unable to move. He offered to help get my foot loose. I did not think it was appropriate for him to touch me, but he insisted it was the best option available at the time. Ellie, when he grasped my foot I felt like it was on fire. I know I was blushing from toe to head. He explained what he was doing and I was trying to pay attention but looking down at him made me so dizzy. He has the thickest, curliest, black hair of anyone I have ever seen. I must have fainted because the next thing I knew, I was on the floor. More accurately, the duke was laid out on the floor and I was sitting on his chest."

"My stars, Emmie, you get in more messes. What did he say?"

"For me to get off him, of course. I rolled to his side and he stood up immediately. When he reached down to help me stand, he slipped and was on the ground again—and I was sitting in his lap."

"Oh, my! Talk about inappropriate. Was he angry?"

"No. We both started laughing."

"You are lucky no one saw you alone in such a compromising position."

"We were seen. By none other than Lady Cecelia. She was livid to find us together after the duke had practically shoved her out of the library only moments earlier. She accused me of trying to entrap the duke into marriage. She called me a country bumpkin who was trying to become a duchess through a ruse and some other choice words. Her face was bright red. She was so angry."

"Emmie, that could ruin your reputation."

"No, dear cousin, remember, I was found in that position as Miss Eleanor Brown. I am afraid I put your reputation at risk. I am glad Lord Simon was with the real Miss Brown at the time of this adventure. The duke was marvelous. He defended me and made every effort to correct Lady Cecelia's mistaken assumptions. I could not stand there quietly and let her continue to harangue at me. I called her a doxy masquerading as a lady who was jealous she did not think of the library ruse first."

"I am sure that didn't help the situation. Uncle has warned you about being cheeky."

"I was rewarded for my sassy mouth by a slap—hard enough to leave a mark for over an hour. Even after I put a cool cloth on it."

"Emmie, I am so sorry. The duke must have been completely embarrassed by your behavior."

"If he was, he never showed it. He was angry at Lady Cecelia. He stopped her from striking me a second time and offered to carry the books back to my sitting room."

"Emmie, do you care for him? Does he for you?"

"I do not know the answer to either question. I can only tell you I am certain I have made an enemy of Lady Cecelia. She told me I would not want to meet her alone. I think she sees me as a threat to getting what she wants—the Duke of Wallingford."

"Lady Beatrice did say she has her mind set on being his duchess. You need to tread lightly around her. For mercy's sake, do not do anything else to antagonize her."

"I was not trying to attract the duke or aggravate Lady Cecelia. I was simply looking for some books to read to pass the time. Oh, no."

"What else?"

"I think I told the duke I had no interest in marrying. Anyone. Me and my mouth."

****

After dinner, everyone gathered in the gold salon for ratafia, brandy, and a rollicking game of charades. Lady Cecelia missed the meal but came into the room accepting all the sympathy she could garner for her earlier headache. She wasted no time planting herself on the settee next to the duke before anyone else had a chance to approach the area. 'Miss Brown' sat in a large wingback chair next to the settee on the duke's side. The horseback riders had paired together on sofas and settees throughout the room. The rest of the guests filled the vacant chairs.

They did not pick teams or keep score on the game. It was all in good fun to give everyone an opportunity to act out a book or famous person or animal. Laughter rang through the room.

The duke's turn came and he began his miming. It was a person. Apparently someone dressed in a toga giving an oration.

"Plato!" 'Miss Brown' called out.

"That is right, Miss Eleanor. It is your turn." Grey sat back down.

Lady Cecelia leaned forward and whispered in his ear, "I knew it. I was about to guess when I was interrupted by that rube." Grey ignored her.

'Miss Brown' began her mime. It was a book. She held up two fingers indicating the second word. Then she pointed skyward.

"*Wuthering Heights*," Grey guessed jumping to his feet.

"Your Grace is correct." She smiled broadly.

"We seem to be riding the same train of thought tonight, Miss Eleanor." Grey bowed to her and sat down.

'Eleanor' was almost back to her chair when something caused her to stumble. She nearly embarrassed herself by falling on the floor in front of everyone. At the last second, a strong arm wrapped around her waist and righted her. The duke. The heat in her cheeks meant they must be bright red. Their eyes met and she wavered a moment. She could hardly get her breath. He was still holding her.

"Are you hurt?"

"No, Your Grace. Thank you for rescuing me…again."

"What a cow. Miss Brown cannot even walk across the room without falling," Cecelia brayed.

Lady Chelmsford stood and quickly crossed the room until she was almost toe-to-toe with Lady Cecelia. "I hate to be the bearer of bad news but it is growing late. Perhaps it is time for us to all retire for the evening."

"No! We must not stop yet. I have not had my turn," Lady Cecelia loudly protested.

Lady Chelmsford's tone was sharp as she lowered her voice and spoke directly to her unhappy guest, "I believe you have embarrassed yourself and others enough for one evening. It is time for you to leave the room." Caroline's coal-black eyes glinted with anger.

Lady Cecelia stood up, spun around, and stomped out of the room in a most unladylike fashion. Her embarrassed sister, Beatrice, said good night and followed close behind. Within minutes the room was nearly empty.

Caroline turned to her brother. "Your Grace, I believe Miss Brown is sufficiently recovered to stand on her own two feet now," she said with a smile.

Grey hadn't realized he still had his hands around Eleanor's waist—what a tiny waist it was. He dropped his hands to his side. "I hope I did not make you uncomfortable, Miss Brown."

"On the contrary, Your Grace. I am very thankful you were there to keep me from upending." She smiled. "I am not usually so clumsy. I cannot imagine what I tripped on." She scoured the floor around her.

"It was not a what, my dear. It was a who," her cousin said quietly.

"Lady Cecelia?" Grey asked. "But why would she be so cruel?"

Caroline laughed. "My darling brother, she is jealous of Miss Eleanor after the library episode earlier today. Cecelia is trying her best to make Eleanor look less attractive to you. The joke is on her. She expected her victim to hit the floor, not fall into the arms of the man Cecelia herself is stalking."

"But I did not do it on purpose," 'Eleanor' protested.

"We know you are the victim here. Do not give it another thought. I am just thankful you were not harmed. I would never be able to look your aunt in the eye if I had allowed something to happen to one of her treasured nieces."

"I am also thankful you were unhurt. I feel like the vitriol Lady Cecelia is raining down on you is my fault. I had no idea how determined she is to be a duchess or how backwardly she would try to accomplish her goal," the duke said.

"Not a duchess, Your Grace, *your* duchess," 'Emmeline' said. "Come, sweet cousin, it is time for us to retire as well."

Eleanor and Emmeline left the salon.

"Caro, is Lady Emmeline correct? Has Lady Cecelia set her cap for me?"

"Think about it, Grey. You are the one who told me she practically glued herself to you earlier today. She does meet your criteria of a beauty with a very generous father."

Grey shook his head. "Sister dear, I believe I am going to have to expand my definition of the ideal Duchess of Wallingford. No amount of money could make me listen to her hyena's laugh for the rest of my life. I would be certain to go stark raving mad. She is definitely a beauty on the outside, but I believe her soul is as black as the ace of spades."

"I fear you are right. Lady Emmeline is quite a beauty and has a very generous papa. She seems to be as sweet as she is lovely."

"Yes, but Simon Hartsfield appears to have laid claim to her. Miss Brown is equally beautiful. She is sweet but has a bit of sass to her. I do not know why, but I find her kind of appealing. I am sure life would never be boring with her around." Grey stared off into space as if imagining being married to Miss Brown.

"But it would be a life somewhere other than Wallingford because that cousin is a penniless orphan. Think about it."

"Leave it to me to fall under the spell of the wrong cousin."

"So it is not Lady Cecelia's imagination. You are bewitched by Miss Eleanor Brown."

"I do not believe I said anything out loud and to my matchmaking sister of all people. Yes, I find her charming. Especially compared to the cackling Lady Cecelia Thompson. Do not be marrying me off to her yet. We are not even to Christmas." Grey kissed his sister's cheek. "I expected to be bored this week. I am anything but that. Good night, Caro. Sweet dreams. You have given me something to think about."

****

Maisie helped Emmie and Ellie out of their gowns and into bedclothes. Maisie brushed out Emmeline's long chestnut hair before braiding it for bed while Emmie brushed and braided Eleanor's hair. When they were snuggled in their bed, Maisie doused the lantern and left the room.

"You are not going to sleep yet, are you?" Emmie asked.

"No. How could I? Who knew how exciting a game of charades could be with almost strangers? You and the duke did seem to be reading each other's minds."

Emmie laughed. "The two books I dropped in the library were Plato's *Dialogues* and *Wuthering Heights*. I guess we were thinking about being in the library together earlier today."

"Why that borders on cheating! It certainly explains how quickly you both guessed the other's mime before the rest of us had a clue what the answer was. Emmie, I think he likes you. Why else would he be thinking about the library? I heard his sister's brother-in-law, Paul Winter, talking when we were riding. The duke needs a wife with a big dowry to maintain his estate."

"Despite his financial state, I think the duke likes *me*. Remember, I am playing Eleanor. He seems

51

interested in this little church mouse orphan Eleanor Brown. I am so glad you were willing to trade places with me, Ellie. And Lord Simon seems increasingly besotted with Lady Emmeline when he does not need a pound of her dowry. Papa may be pleasantly surprised when he arrives after Christmas."

"Please be careful around Lady Cecelia. Anyone who would intentionally try to hurt you in front of all those witnesses may do something much worse given the opportunity to find you alone."

"I will. I love you, Ellie. Good night."

"I love you, Emmie. Good night."

Chapter Six

No one joined Emmeline and Eleanor at breakfast. The server said they were the first guests he'd seen all morning. After breakfast, they got their cloaks and bonnets and went exploring.

The weather was cooperating. There was only a slight nip in the air. The bailey around the castle had more tents and carnival games set up. A few of them would be open later today. The full carnival and the Christmas celebration for Winterhaven and its village would kick off tomorrow.

They walked around taking in all the displays and trying to decide what to do for the day. Lord Simon spied 'Lady Emmeline' and raced across the grounds to wish her good morning and inquire how she slept. Neither of them noticed when her cousin slipped away.

'Miss Brown' slowly opened the door to the hothouse. She immediately peeled out of her cape and bonnet. It was nearly tropical in the glass house from the large number of fire pots burning. She wandered around looking at the exotic plants. The castle gardener, Hobbs, came over and asked if she had any questions. They were bent over an unusual type of peony when a deep voice startled her.

"Miss Brown, I did not know you were interested in plants. It is kind of a hobby of mine," the duke said.

"Oh, yes, Your Grace. I love seeing the variety of

flowers that are created from grafting different kinds together. It has always fascinated me. This hothouse is a treasure trove of amazing plants. Hobbs has been giving me a tour of his arena. He has done some amazing things."

"Would you like to see the surprise I brought for my sister's Christmas gift?" Grey asked proudly.

"I should love to."

The duke led her to a corner of the hothouse. She had to concentrate to ignore the pleasant warmth of his hand on her arm and his unique masculine scent. Several sheets were hung from a line running across one corner of the building. A sign on the sheets said: *Keep Out! This especially means you, Caroline!*

"Your Grace, are you sure it is all right for us to go behind the curtain?"

The duke laughed. "Absolutely, I am the one who put up the sign. My twin sister tends to be a bit nosy, especially when she knows I have a special surprise for her. She is worse than a small child about not wanting to wait until Christmas for her gifts." He pulled the sheet back and motioned for 'Miss Brown' to enter.

"Darling, I thought you would never get here. I swear I am about to melt in this hot box," Lady Cecelia said as she turned around wearing a low-cut, tight-fitting gown and her arms open wide.

'Miss Brown' stepped back away from the unexpected visitor and into the duke's outstretched arms. She quickly excused herself and moved behind him.

"What on earth is *she* doing here?" Cecelia screeched.

"Miss Brown is here at my invitation. The more

pertinent question is what are *you* doing here?" Grey demanded.

"Is it not obvious, my darling duke? I have been waiting for you for over an hour. You took your sweet time coming out to check on your precious bush this morning. You usually come here first thing."

"Can you not read? The sign says 'Keep out!' What part of the message is unclear?"

"I was simply trying to find a quiet, out of the way place where you and I could meet privately so we could get to know one another better. I am afraid we have gotten off on the wrong foot. Would you not agree, Your Grace?" Cecelia smiled at him batting her eyes.

"Yes," the duke said tersely.

"Good, then send the country bumpkin away." Cecelia waved 'Eleanor' away from her.

"Lady Cecelia, yes, I agree we got off on the wrong foot. However, you have done nothing to merit any private time with me. I would appreciate it if you left the hothouse. You interrupted something Miss Brown and I were in the middle of doing." Grey shooed her away.

"But you cannot dismiss me as if I were only a nobody like her."

"First, she is not a nobody. Second, I am a duke, I may dismiss whomever I chose. Third, I do not want your company." Grey extended his hand to 'Miss Brown' and led her past Cecelia to two large rosebushes in the back corner of the hothouse.

Cecelia stood without moving. She seemed to be in shock. She sobbed covering her face with her hands. Then looked to see if the duke was watching. No response from him. She wailed louder. No response.

The next time she cried, the gardener came into the sectioned off area.

"Your Grace, may I be of assistance?"

"Thank you, Hobbs. Please take this lady back to the keep. She has apparently lost her way."

Cecelia caterwauled all the way out of the hothouse, but meekly followed Hobbs.

"Now, where were we?" Grey asked.

"You were explaining about the four types of roses you have bred together to create this beautiful plant in front of me. How long has the process taken, Your Grace?"

"This is the result of six years of tending and training. Grafting to create a new species is a painfully slow process. Lots of misses before you achieve what you are looking for. I hope Caroline likes it."

"How could she not? It is truly unique. I have never seen a rose bloom with four distinct rings of color like this. I am sure she will treasure it."

"I have submitted it to the Royal Botanical Society as a new type of rose. I named it The Lady Caroline Winter Rose. I have not heard back from them yet."

"What an amazing gift. Even if they do not recognize the achievement, Lady Chelmsford will be honored. You are a very thoughtful and talented man, Your Grace."

"Thank you for letting me tell you about it, Miss Eleanor. I wanted to see another woman's reaction before I gave it to Caroline. You have convinced me she will love it. Shall we?"

The duke helped 'Eleanor' into her cape and bonnet, then walked her back to the keep where 'Emmeline' was in the entrance hall with Lord Simon.

Lord Simon stepped forward. "We were contemplating another ride this morning in a different direction. Would you two be interested in joining us?"

'Eleanor' looked at the duke who nodded slightly.

"I would love to go. The grounds are so lovely and the snow has held off," 'Eleanor' said.

"I think it would be refreshing," the duke said.

"I hope we are in time to join this party," Lord William said with Lady Beatrice clinging to his arm.

"If my sister is going, then so am I," Lady Cecelia announced as she came down the stairs from the sleeping area. "Paul, will you join us?"

"Excellent idea. Paul knows the trails better than any of us," Grey said.

"It is a nice enough day for a picnic. Do you think Lady Chelmsford would mind if we asked Cook to whip something light up so we do not have to hurry back for lunch?" 'Emmeline' asked.

"I have already done so when I saw the group gathering in the entrance hall," Lady Chelmsford announced as she joined them. "You may leave whenever you are ready. One of my footmen will follow and bring your picnic. Paul, do you remember where the waterfall grotto is?"

"Yes."

"It is a lovely spot for a picnic. If you will guide the group in that direction, I shall have Hudson bring the meal there."

"It would be my pleasure."

The ladies left to gather bonnets and capes to be ready for the ride. Then Paul led them to the stables to select their mounts for the adventure.

The well-marked trail was only wide enough for

two riders to go abreast. In some places, it narrowed to single file. The duke made certain to stay behind Lord Simon and 'Lady Emmeline' and at 'Miss Eleanor's' side. Lord William and Lady Beatrice followed them and Lady Cecelia and Paul brought up the rear. Even with all those people and animals between them, Lady Cecelia's frequent cackle carried over the wind causing Grey to shudder every time he heard it.

By the time they reached the waterfall, Hudson had arrived and laid out their feast. He explained there was a shorter path large enough to accommodate the carriage which allowed him to reach the destination before them.

The sun came out and took every vestige of cold out of the still air. The pond at the bottom of the waterfall twinkled as the sunlight bounced off its surface. Near the base of the falls the water sprayed up in mists that showed rainbows twinkling in the bright sunshine. It was breathtaking.

They sat down on the ground on beautiful Scottish plaid blankets Hudson had spread out far enough away from the spray to be comfortable. Each couple claimed a blanket basically in the same order as they had ridden. When everyone was seated Lady Cecelia insisted that Lady Beatrice change places with her since Cecelia didn't want staring into the sun to give her another sick headache. Her sister reluctantly agreed but was delighted when Lord William moved with her. Paul Winter stayed where he was, so Beatrice was attended by two gentlemen. A scowling Lady Cecelia plopped down on the blanket alone and insisted Hudson attend to her exclusively since none of the other gentlemen were doing so.

After a tasty repast, they decided to explore the grotto behind the waterfall. The duke with 'Miss Brown' on his arm led the way. The path behind the waterfall was quite narrow and slick from the spray. The pool behind the waterfall glistened darkly in the half-light showing through the falls. The walls beneath and around the pool glowed iridescently with sapphire blue and emerald green rocks.

"What are the stones lining the walls?" 'Lady Emmeline' asked.

"The blue is azurite, it is considered a gemstone. The green is fluorite," Paul answered. "When the earl and I were children we were convinced we would be rich if our father would let us strip all the gems off the grotto walls and sell them."

"I am glad he did not allow you to become rich," Lady Beatrice said. "It is too beautiful to disturb. I do not believe I have ever seen anything like it."

The duke cautioned everyone to watch their step. He recommended they move single file holding hands. Much to 'Eleanor's' dismay, Lady Cecelia grabbed hers. They carefully inched their way across the wet ledge. The roar of the falling water made it very hard to hear.

Lady Cecelia yelled, "Look out, Miss Brown. You are about to slip."

'Eleanor' couldn't understand her but stopped and leaned toward Cecelia to see what she had said. Cecelia jerked her hand free from 'Eleanor's' and let loose that infuriating cackle.

"I said you are going to fall!"

Cecelia watched as 'Eleanor' tried to regain her balance. Fortunately, the duke was strong enough to hold her upright from her other side.

'Eleanor' was furious. She turned to look at Cecelia who was holding Beatrice's hand and smirking. She turned back to the duke. That harpy wasn't worth the effort to get angry.

Splash! Water lapped onto the ledge and the hem of 'Eleanor's' gown. Lady Cecelia's head bobbed atop the surface of the pool. The grotto pool was only five feet deep so she could easily keep her nose above water if she leaned back. Echoing screams made it clear that her mouth was above water.

Grey led the party out of the grotto while assuring Lady Cecelia they would come back to rescue her once the other ladies were safe. Grey, Simon, William, Paul, and Hudson came back along the ledge single file and hoisted the sodden woman out of the pool. She nearly pulled them into the drink with her uncontrolled thrashing. Her gown was so heavy, it took all of them with a rope around the lady's waist to hoist her up onto the ledge. She swore she was too shaken to stand on her own, much less walk, and insisted the duke, and only the duke, carry her out of the cave.

Grey hefted Cecelia over his shoulder like a wet sack of feed, and hauled her into the sunlight screaming and kicking the entire way. He unceremoniously dumped her into the carriage, piled the picnic blankets on top of her, then instructed Hudson to take her back to the castle with all haste to keep her from getting pneumonia.

Lady Beatrice watched the rescue with her hand at her mouth, unsuccessfully trying to suppress a laugh. "I cannot imagine why Cecelia thought it was a good idea to let go of my hand at that particular moment. It is lucky for you, Eleanor, that you are so surefooted. She could have pulled you in with her."

"Oh, she was never going to pull me in. She had dropped my hand a few minutes earlier before she tried to push me in the pool," 'Eleanor' said matter-of-factly.

"I apologize for my sister's behavior. If it is any consolation, I am sure the duke did not carry her out of the grotto as she had envisioned. Her idea was undoubtedly more romantic like him sweeping her into his arms while she rested her head on his chest." Beatrice laughed. Emmeline and Eleanor joined her.

The gentlemen rejoined the ladies and asked what was so funny.

"Nothing but a little girl talk," Beatrice assured them.

Chapter Seven

Lady Cecelia did not join them for tea. Beatrice reported she was still trying to get warm after her tumble into the grotto pool and the cool ride home. It was probably for the best since she would not have wanted to be the subject of jest.

Lady Chelmsford announced there was a small entertainment planned before dinner. Her sons and their nanny had a short Christmas program prepared. Everyone agreed to come down in two hours to the green parlor where the piano was. Then they retired to rest from their morning's adventures.

"Is it not lovely that Lady Caroline does not hide her children away in the nursery? Stephen and Oliver are very bright, well behaved, and very comfortable conversing with adults," Eleanor said.

"They probably get more exposure to adults than most children do," Emmeline said.

"Lady Caroline said they would be needing a governess in the new year. Do you think they would consider me—once they know who I really am?"

"Ellie, do not be ridiculous. Do you not think Viscount Simon Summerly has other plans for you?"

"I am not certain. I know he says he does not need a dowered wife, but I am not comfortable he will appreciate our little deception. I am not only without a dowry, I am without family connections."

"The next time you are with him, look in his eyes when he is watching you. The man is totally smitten with you…whoever you are…whatever name you use. I am positive the Earl and Countess Chelmsford will be looking elsewhere for a governess for their sons."

****

Oliver and Simon were dressed in matching suits. They looked like the miniature lords they were with black brocade cutaway coats, buff-colored breeches, tall black boots, and Christmas red vests. The buckles on their boots shone almost as brightly as their eyes. Nanny was dressed in a modest, long-sleeved, red velvet gown with cream-colored lace along the neckline. She took a seat at the piano once everyone was assembled in the salon. Even Lady Cecelia had come for the entertainment. The boys stood in front of the piano, held hands, then bowed.

"Thank you for joining us. I am Oliver Winter and this is my younger brother, Stephen. Nanny is playing the piano for us. We hope you enjoy our performance."

They sang "The First Noel" so sweetly you could imagine the town of Bethlehem in front of you. Then a cheery "Deck the Halls" and "Joy to the World".

Stephen stepped forward. "If you would like to sing along with us, please do. We shall not mind a bit."

Nanny launched into a rollicking rendition of "God Rest Ye Merry Gentlemen" on the piano and everyone in the audience sang along. The entire group joined in the singing for over an hour. Then Lady Caroline requested "The Twelve Days of Christmas" with each person or group of people taking a specific day to sing. It took a few minutes for everyone to get their assignments.

Oliver and Stephen kicked off day one of the partridge in a pear tree.

Lady Caroline and her brother took the two turtle doves.

Lord Richard and his brother's baritone voices sang about three French hens.

Lady Cornelia and Lord Edward combined to do four calling birds.

Lady Cecelia insisted that she be the only singer on day five because she had the perfect voice for the five golden rings.

Lord Simon asked for 'Lady Emmeline' to help him with six geese-a-laying.

Lord and Lady Castleberry claimed seven swans-a-swimming.

Lord and Lady Bollingwood asked for eight maids-a-milking.

Lady Beatrice and Lord William sang beautifully about nine ladies dancing.

'Miss Eleanor' soloed for ten lords-a-leaping.

The Duke of Wingate's bass voice sang eleven pipers piping.

The Dowager Countess Chelmsford, Lady Margaret, and her sister, Lady Agatha Crowley wanted twelve drummers drumming so they could sing the least.

It was a great deal of fun. Oliver and Stephen had the biggest job of repeating the partridge in the pear tree. Caroline and Grey harmonized beautifully as did Richard and Paul. Cornelia and Edward had clearly sung together before. Cecelia did have a hauntingly beautiful soprano voice for day five and was clearly proud of her solo. Simon and his partner sounded like old hands on their duet as did the Castleberrys and Bollingwoods. Beatrice and William kept missing their cue to jump in with the nine ladies dancing. Probably because they were too busy gazing into one another's eyes instead of listening to the music. 'Miss Brown's' voice was robust and beautiful. The Duke of Wingate, the Dowager Countess, and Lady Crowley ended the song perfectly.

They stood in a circle and sang "We Wish You a Merry Christmas" led by Oliver and Stephen in the middle. Then the boys led all the guests to the Great Hall where a surprise waited. While they were singing the castle woodsmen had installed a giant pine tree in one corner of the room. Scaffolding had been erected around the tree to assist with reaching the higher branches.

The guests helped string popcorn and holly berries to make festive garlands for the Christmas tree. Lady Caroline brought out boxes filled with fragile glass ornaments to hang on higher branches. The boys worked with Nanny to cut out snowflakes to hang on the tree and made paper chains which they draped across the lower branches.

The ladies—Cecelia, Beatrice, Eleanor, and Emmeline—walked up onto the scaffolding from the stairs. They each were responsible for one side of the massive tree. They draped garland around the tallest branches and hung smaller ornaments at intervals around the perimeter. Beatrice and 'Lady Emmeline' finished their sides and carefully made their way down the steps. Lady Chelmsford walked partway up the stairs and handed a beautiful angel tree topper to 'Miss Brown' who was closest to the steps to finish the top level decorating.

To reach the angel's perch atop the tree she had to move past Cecelia on the narrow scaffolding. As she carefully edged around Cecelia, the woman moved suddenly tripping 'Miss Brown'. A scream echoed through the hall. The angel flew into the air as 'Eleanor' lost her footing and fell from the scaffolding. Cecelia caught the ornament in mid-air. The duke ran to the base of the scaffolding and snatched 'Miss Brown' in mid-flight before she fell all the way to the ground.

He held her securely around the waist and bent to carefully set her on her feet. She couldn't stop shaking. He put his arm around her shoulders and held her close.

"You are on the ground. Do you hurt anywhere?"

"Luckily, I think only my pride is damaged. Once again, Your Grace, you have rescued me from great harm. I do not understand how I continue to be so clumsy. Thank you."

"I believe you had help, cousin." 'Emmeline' had rushed over to her.

"I am glad you were not hurt but you must stop falling into my arms. If it continues to happen so frequently, people will talk." The duke winked at her, then released her from his embrace.

'Eleanor's' cheeks became instantly warm.

Cecelia remained on the scaffolding, becoming distressed that everyone was huddled around 'Miss Brown' and she was unwatched.

"Excuse me," she yelled. "I am going to put the angel atop the tree."

Grey never took his eyes off 'Miss Brown.'

There was a weak round of applause when the angel was securely in place. Cecelia strode across the scaffolding and down the steps.

Lord and Lady Chelmsford placed gaily wrapped small gifts with bright colored ribbons on the lower branches snuggled against the lush green needles of the tree. The staff dismantled the scaffolding and stairs. The guests stood back to admire their handiwork. It was a beautiful tree with exquisite decorations.

The butler stepped to the top of the stairs and announced, "Dinner is served." The boys and Nanny said "Good night" and retired to the nursery for their dinner.

Lady Chelmsford whispered something to her husband and rushed ahead of everyone to the dining room. She had Lady Cecelia by the arm. They were leaving as the rest of the guests entered the dining room. Cecelia began to speak but the countess hurried her out of the room. After the remaining guests were seated, Lady Chelmsford returned to the dining room and announced that Lady Cecelia had another of her headaches and sent her regrets that she would not be well enough to attend dinner.

There was only the briefest of lulls in the conversations after Lady Chelmsford's announcement, then the merriment of the singing and tree decorating carried over to lively dinner conversation. Grey continued to observe 'Miss Brown' hoping she was truly unhurt. He was relieved his sister had removed Lady Cecelia from his presence so he didn't have to listen to her cackle after almost maiming 'Miss Brown'.

Tomorrow the carnival would begin and the Christmas feast for the village would be held in the Great Hall. They all needed to be well rested for the coming day's full schedule of festivities.

****

"Ellie, you and Simon have perfect harmony together. Was that not fun?"

"I was afraid I would be unable to sing standing so close to him. Did you notice he rested his hand on my back? I hope it was not improper to allow him to touch me. Feeling the warmth of his presence made me feel more confident and able to sing even if it took my breath away at first."

"You were not improper at all. Do you still think you will need to be looking for a position in the new year?"

"No, you are right, Emmie. He does look like he loves me. Those blue eyes seem to get brighter when he looks at me. I am sorry you did not get paired with the duke. His marvelous baritone would have been beautiful with your voice."

"I suspect Lady Chelmsford claimed the right to sing with her brother to prevent another embarrassing incident with the grasping Lady Cecelia, although I am not sure she would have given up her solo even to sing with *her* duke. After the hothouse this morning and the grotto this afternoon, I should have been more careful on the scaffolding. I am positive she deliberately tripped me. If it were not for the duke, I could have been killed after falling from such a height. There is no telling what Cecelia might do if I were to get too close to her targeted husband-to-be again. The woman is completely obsessed."

"Lady Caroline said she was afraid she made you a target by handing the tree topper to you instead of Cecelia."

"It was not her fault. No one else has a devious

enough mind to stay ahead of whatever Lady Cecelia Thompson has planned. I am exhausted. How can one day be both marvelous and disastrous simultaneously?"

"It was wild. Perhaps tomorrow will be tamer. Have sweet dreams, Emmie."

"You too, Ellie."

Chapter Eight

While Emmeline and Eleanor were having breakfast and visiting with Lady Caroline and the duke, Oliver and Stephen raced into the room. Both were talking at once.

"Uncle Grey, please come with us. There are all kinds of wild animals outside. And rides and music. Please. Papa cannot come with us right now."

"My sons are not usually so rude. I apologize," Lady Caroline said, barely suppressing a smile.

Oliver went to her side. "Good morning, Mother dear. Good morning, Miss Eleanor and Lady Emmeline. We are not trying to be rude. We are just excited. Have you seen what is out in the bailey?"

"No apologies are necessary," 'Eleanor' said. "I have been anxious to get out there myself. It promises to be a marvelous carnival."

"Then you come with us too," Stephen said. "Uncle Grey will not mind, will you?" He looked at his uncle.

"I should be delighted to escort Miss Brown and the two young gentlemen. Lady Emmeline, will you also join us?" Grey stood.

'Emmeline' started to respond but Lord Summerly entered the breakfast room. "Thank you, Your Grace. I believe I shall have another cup of tea. You four go and have fun. I shall be out later."

The boys each grabbed one of their uncle's hands. Grey stopped and had Oliver take Stephen's hand, putting the younger boy between them. He held out his free hand in 'Eleanor's' direction. "Miss Brown? You may want to hold on so we do not lose you in the throng outside."

She happily took the offered hand. The duke's touch sent shots of warmth running up her arm. They escaped out of the keep and onto the bailey, which now was filled with a full-fledged carnival spilling across the drawbridge into the large meadow in front of the castle.

Calliope music filled the air emanating from a merry-go-round with beautifully carved animals—horses, lambs, unicorns, bears, tigers, elephants, even geese. The boys wanted to ride it before they looked at anything else. Oliver selected a ferocious-looking Bengal tiger to ride and his brother wanted to ride the larger elephant—but not alone.

"Miss Brown, how would you like to ride an elephant with me?" Stephen shyly asked.

"I would be delighted, if I can figure out how to ride the animal side saddle. My skirt is not suitable for spanning the girth of this beast."

"Let me help." The duke put Stephen on the pachyderm first at the front where he could hold on to the saddle horn, then he lifted 'Eleanor' and gently placed her sitting side saddle behind his nephew.

"Miss Brown, hold on to me. I will never let you fall," Stephen said.

"I shall ride standing up to make sure no one slips from their mount." Grey stayed between the elephant and tiger. His hand rested on her hip ensuring she stayed atop the pachyderm. She wrapped both arms around Stephen's waist as he requested, knowing the duke would keep her in place. She couldn't look at him for fear her expression would betray what her heart was saying with every single beat. *Love me. Love me.*

The boys and 'Eleanor' slid off their mounts. His nephews pulled Grey off the merry-go-round and down the concourse with her holding on to the duke's elbow.

There was a man with exotic animals in a pen. A full-sized African elephant with gigantic ears and ivory tusks that the boys fed. Its trunk reached out and curled around the peanuts they held in their hands. There was a black and white striped pony they called a zebra. The boys petted its velvety nose. The smelly, shaggy, brown animal with two humps on his back—a camel—spat at Oliver when he tried to pet it and it nipped at Stephen with big yellow teeth.

The man who owned the menagerie walked around the pen with a long-armed, long-tailed, black and white spider monkey perched on his shoulder. It screeched loudly nearly the entire time. It had an eerily familiar laugh.

Stephen tugged on her skirt with his free hand. "Miss Eleanor, I think that monkey sounds just like Lady Cecelia when she laughs. Do you?"

She tried hard not to giggle and quickly looked at the duke to see if he'd heard his nephew's spot-on observation.

"Perhaps a little, but you should never say so to Lady Cecelia," she responded.

"Why not?" Stephen asked.

"You might hurt her feelings. You would not want to do that, would you?"

"No, but it is the truth. I do not understand why she would feel bad for sounding like a monkey. I should like it very much if someone told me I laughed like one. He is funny."

The duke stopped and bent down to Stephen's level. "You will learn as you grow up that ladies, especially refined ones like Lady Cecelia, do not always like the same things little boys do. In fact, most of the time, if it is something you like, they probably would not care for it at all. Do you understand?"

"I guess." He thought for a moment. "I am very sorry, Miss Brown. I hope I did not hurt your feelings."

"Why are you apologizing to me?"

"For asking you to ride an elephant with me. I thought you would like it because I wanted to do it. It was a lot of fun for a little boy like me."

She bent and hugged him. "No apology is needed. I loved being on the elephant with you. It was a lot of fun for a grown woman like me too. I will let you in on a little secret. My Papa told me often that I was not a very well-behaved young lady, so I shall probably like the exact same things you do, even if Lady Cecelia would not."

Oliver patted his younger brother on the back. "Do not try to figure it out, Stephen. Women are very complicated."

'Eleanor' shot a look at their surprised uncle. "Where do you think he heard those words of wisdom, Your Grace?"

He recovered, smiled, and said, "I hope from me as the child speaks words of great truth."

They resumed the stroll across the bailey hand-in-hand laughing with each step.

The delicious aroma of baked goods wafted on the breeze. One of the bakers had put a batch of hand pies out on the table to cool as they walked by.

"Stop here," 'Eleanor' requested. "Breathe in deeply, boys. That is what heaven smells like." The three of them stood close to the edge of the table breathing in the sweet, fruity aroma. The duke stood watching them with a broad grin on his face.

"Would it not be even better to taste a little bit of heaven?" Grey asked.

"Mother does not like us to eat between meals," Oliver announced solemnly.

"Ah, but it is a special holiday. Maybe your mother does not have to know," his uncle said.

"But, Uncle Grey, Mother says not telling something is as big a lie as telling a story. It is not a good thing to do," Stephen said.

"You are right, Stephen. I fear I have forgotten some of the rules of being a boy. I know the solution. As a duke, I outrank all of you and I order us all to have a pie right now."

'Miss Eleanor' reached for a pie. "Your mother would not want you to disobey your uncle and especially not to refuse to do what a duke commands." Grey paid the baker for their treats.

"I like your orders, Uncle Grey. You are a very good duke," Oliver said handing a pie to his brother and taking one for himself.

"And you will be a wonderful father," she whispered.

"I hope so."

"Oh, Your Grace, I did not know you could hear me."

"But I did. At this moment, I am delighted to simply be a wonderful uncle and a very good duke. Let us go look at the side show. Stay together. We cannot hold hands while we are eating pie."

The duke led the little tribe to the other side of the bailey where there was a side show barker making a pitch to the increasing crowd. The boys stood in rapt attention when a bearded fat lady waddled across the stage.

Next, a trainer with a whip brought a tall man on a chain that looped around his waist and wrapped around his wrists. His hair was black and looked like it was woven into place with feathers and even shells. His teeth were filed to points like a vicious animal's would be. There were colorful tattoos covering every visible inch of his scantily clad body. He had a bone running through his nose and a necklace of human teeth around his neck. The trainer said he was a cannibal from the South Pacific islands.

The cannibal growled and tugged at his chains, almost toppling his handler. He lunged toward the edge of the stage near the boys making a loud guttural sound. Stephen stepped forward and growled back at him. Oliver tossed him a piece of pie, which the cannibal caught in mid-air and gobbled down in one bite much to the delight of onlookers.

The next stage had a blindfolded brightly dressed gypsy man who threw knives at a woman he said was his wife. She stood very still on the opposite end of the platform. He pulled a knife from his belt, turned, and quickly threw it. The whole crowd gasped with the release of each knife. Then clapped when no blood was shed.

While they were watching the performance, a woman crept up behind them, put her hands over the duke's eyes, and said "Guess who?" then cackled.

The boys burst into giggles. 'Eleanor' could barely suppress her own. The duke reached up and removed the hands saying, "Lady Cecelia, are you enjoying the carnival this morning?"

"I only got here a few minutes ago. Looks like I missed a sweet treat."

The boys had fruit filling smeared across their faces and on their hands. Grey got out his handkerchief and wiped away the debris as best he could. He looked at 'Eleanor' who had a tiny bit of fruit in the corner of her mouth. "Pardon me, Miss Eleanor. You need some clean up too." He reached over with a clean corner of his handkerchief and removed the offending crumbs.

"Your Grace, what is next?" Lady Cecelia asked trying to take the duke's arm. He carefully removed her hand and grasped a nephew's hand in each of his, then Stephen offered his hand to 'Miss Brown'.

"You are welcome to follow us," Grey said.

"Never mind. I just remembered I have an appointment to go strolling with Paul Winter. I shall see you later at the feast in the Great Hall." Cecelia retreated to the keep.

A strolling juggler stopped and gave Oliver an impromptu lesson. The boy was quite coordinated as long as he only had three items to juggle. When the fourth pin was added to the mix, they all fell to the ground. The man was part of a team of acrobats who took the stage doing back flips, walking on their hands, and juggling flaming torches.

They ended their act by building a human pyramid

and asked for a small member of the audience to be at the top. Stephen eagerly scrambled onto the stage and one of the acrobats lifted him to the very top of the human pile. Then they told him to jump off and he did so fearlessly, landing in his uncle's arms as the base of the pyramid flattened.

"It is lucky Lady Caroline did not witness that feat," 'Eleanor' said. "She would be worried to death."

"They are boys, Miss Eleanor. Boys do dangerous things and take risks. It is how they are made. I did many daring things as a child and lived to tell about it. I know you do not have any brothers, but have you any male cousins?"

"No, Your Grace. I was raised with Lady Emmeline. Two girls. No other close cousins."

"My sister will not be surprised Stephen is so eager and brave. She wanted to be a boy growing up. It made her angry to have to stay inside doing ladylike things like embroidery and knitting when she wanted to be running like wild men with Thomas and me. It surprises me how much she mollycoddles her boys considering what a daredevil she was as a child."

"I never would have believed she had those tendencies. She is the perfectly mannered countess now. I guess you never know."

"Looks are sometimes quite deceiving." His coal-black eyes stared into hers. "For instance, there is a bit of spice and sass behind the vicar's daughter mask you wear, Miss Brown, if you do not mind the observation."

Did he know who she really was?

"No, Your Grace, I do not mind. As we have already established, you outrank the rest of us. You may observe out loud whatever you wish." She batted her eyes in an exaggerated manner.

"Exactly what I am talking about," Grey muttered under his breath.

They strolled across the drawbridge into the meadow where preparations had started for the first of four donkey races. The first heat was for boys six to eight. The little gray donkeys resisted being saddled. They kicked up their heels and brayed wildly. One even bit the man trying to cinch its saddle.

"Uncle Grey, I am six. I could be in the race, do you not agree?" Oliver asked hopefully.

"I happen to know you will not be six for another three weeks, but I think you are close enough for it to count. I know you can ride horses. Have you ever ridden a donkey?"

"No, sir, but should it not be pretty much the same?"

"Mostly, except donkeys can be wilder and meaner. They are more likely to buck than any of your ponies. They might even try to bite you. You could fall off."

"It is all right, Uncle Grey. They are closer to the ground than any of my ponies. I will not get hurt," he said confidently.

"Surely, Lady Caroline would not approve this," 'Eleanor' said.

"But Uncle Grey does," the duke said.

Grey paid the small entrance fee and walked onto the makeshift track to help Oliver select his mount. Stephen stayed glued to 'Eleanor's' side with eyes wide open.

"Miss Brown, do you think when I grow up to be six I shall be as brave as my brother?" Stephen asked.

"I am certain you shall. You were brave enough to be on the top of the pyramid. And when Uncle Grey is around to help you, how could you be anything else?"

Five boys, some smaller and some taller than Oliver, lined up next to their mounts. Each was allowed to have an adult help them into the saddle of the racing donkey they had selected. The announcer explained where the markers for the short track were and that the winner would be the first rider to complete the loop still on the donkey's back. Riders falling all the way to the ground were disqualified.

"Gentlemen, mount your steeds!" the announcer called.

Those donkeys did not want to be ridden. They bucked and twisted immediately upon feeling extra weight on their backs. Oliver held the saddle and reins tightly using both hands. The wide-eyed expression on his face was one of pure terror and simultaneous joy. When the animal calmed down, Oliver broke into a broad grin. Grey stepped back to stand with 'Eleanor' and Stephen taking one in each hand.

"Gentlemen, you will start on three. One. Two. Three." The starting gun fired. "They are off!"

A dark gray donkey bucked twice. When its rider refused to be discouraged, the animal sat down like a large dog with his forelegs extended. The boy kept goading the animal hoping it would run. It did not.

One animal ran across the middle of the oval and over the barrel on the far side with its rider hollering and hanging on for dear life.

Three animals began running the proper course, including Oliver's. Halfway around the track, one of the donkeys stopped abruptly sending its rider sailing over its head onto the dirt track.

Now it was a two-man race. The opponent screamed, drove his heels into the animal's stomach, and slapped its neck with the reins trying to get more speed from the little beast. Oliver leaned low over his donkey's neck and stroked it while coaxing the animal with sweet words. He was rewarded with a burst of speed in the last half of the race. Oliver and his light gray donkey flew across the finish line an entire length ahead of the competition.

'Eleanor' jumped up and down and danced in a little circle holding hands with Stephen and Grey. "We won! We won!" She kissed Stephen's cheek and then the duke's before she realized what she'd done. She immediately dropped his hand. "I apologize, Your Grace."

"I am certain my brother needs no apology for getting a kiss from a beautiful woman," Lady Caroline said from behind them.

Oliver slid off the donkey and came running with his prize—a loving cup filled with sugared almonds—in hand. "Oh, Mother, did you see me? I won. Uncle Grey put me on the donkey and I won!"

Caroline hugged her son. "You were marvelous. Tell me, what did you say to your donkey that made him run so hard at the end?"

"I promised him I would sneak two carrots from Cook as a special treat for him. I guess he really likes carrots."

"You will not have to sneak them. I am sure Cook will be happy to share her larder with a winning donkey. I came to get you boys for lunch but it appears you have already been eating." She wiped a bit of fruit off Stephen's face.

"We had to, Mother," Oliver said.

"We had no choice about it," Stephen said.

"No choice about eating pie? I have to hear this explanation." Caroline took a boy in each hand. "We will give Miss Eleanor and Uncle Grey a break from children for a bit. Come with me, we shall get the carrots and reward your donkey, then have a proper lunch. You are welcome to come in to eat anytime." Caroline winked at her brother.

Chapter Nine

"Are you hungry? Would you like to go in for lunch?" 'Eleanor' asked the duke.

"After our meal-spoiling treat, I think I can stave off hunger pains a little longer. Do you want to walk the rest of the grounds to see what other dangerous things there are to do?" the duke asked with his eyes glistening mischievously. He placed her hand on his arm as they walked.

The Romany—gypsies—had parked their colorful, elaborately carved vardos on the far side of the meadow where the races were held. Many had tables laden with their craftwork in front of their wagons. Beautiful hammered silver and gold jewelry, some with sparkling jewels set in them. Exquisitely hand tooled leather saddles. Woven, colorful, silky shawls with long fringe. There was even a glassblower at work creating vases and bowls while you watched.

"It is all so beautiful. Luckily I have no money to spend. I would not be able to decide what most caught my fancy."

"They certainly have lots of talented members in their caravan," Grey agreed. "They usually join the feast and dancing later. They are particularly mesmerizing dancers."

"Look, a fortune teller. Would you come with me to have your future revealed?"

"I think it is a lot of mystical rot. But I will accompany you. You should not go alone into a strange, dark tent. Who knows what trouble you could find yourself in."

"Thank you, Your Grace."

Grey pulled the tent flap aside. It took a minute for their eyes to adjust to the sharp contrast between outside and inside. The interior of the tent was lit by a single candle on a table next to a crystal orb resting on a red velvet pillow. A brightly patterned kerchief covered the head of a beautiful Romany woman with cinnamon-colored skin and jet-black hair and eyes. Her bright yellow blouse revealed her bare shoulders. Large golden hoop earrings hung from her ear lobes and delicate gold chains wrapped around her neck multiple times. She beckoned them in. Bracelets jingled together on her arm. Four rings on each hand gleamed in the candlelight.

"You wish to know what your future holds?" she asked with a thick accent.

'Eleanor' hesitated. She looked at the duke. "Maybe we should not do this. Do I really want to know?"

"How much for a reading for the lady?" Grey asked. The woman replied and the duke passed the coins into her outstretched palm.

"Give me your hand, miss. Take a deep breath. Relax."

The woman's hand was warm and calloused. She began humming. Her eyes rolled back in her head. She seemed in a trance. 'Eleanor' reached for Grey with her other hand. She looked at him. He shrugged and patted her hand. As suddenly as the Rom had left their presence, she opened her eyes and smiled at them.

"What I see for you is the true love. Deep and forever love. And many children. You will have strong, daring boys and soft, sweet girls. You two will have a long and very happy life together."

"Oh, you misunderstood. We are not together," 'Eleanor' quickly corrected the seer.

"I did not misread you. Yes. You are together. If not yet, you will be. It is your destiny. You are both trying to keep love away, but it is always there waiting to burst into your hearts and souls. It will win. It always does. First, you must have total truth between you. Then your love will never die. Trust me. I know about these things."

'Eleanor' began to protest again. The woman hushed her.

"But beware. There is one within this castle who wishes to do you harm, my lady. A blonde woman who covets the man at your side. She wishes to be rid of you and to steal this man for her own. You are in grave danger. Sir, you must protect her. Or all my visions will come to naught."

"Thank you," Grey said to the woman and passed her another coin. He gently helped 'Eleanor' up from the chair and led her out of the seer's tent.

"Your Grace, I am sorry to have embarrassed you by having you accompany me into her tent."

"I am not embarrassed, Eleanor."

"But, Your Grace."

"I am becoming a convert. She knew about daring boys and she knows jealous Lady Cecelia is trying to be my bride and she has no love for you. Perhaps fortune telling is not as much rot as I initially believed. I have never actually witnessed it until now," Grey said.

"But, Your Grace. I have no dowry. I am not the woman made to be your duchess. Lady Cecelia has told you so more than once."

"Perhaps you should be calling me Grey now instead of Your Grace. After all, your destiny is to be the mother of my children. Please smile. Otherwise, people looking at us will think I am scolding you."

She peeked at him and smiled broadly. "Yes, Your...Grey. But only when we are alone which properly we should never be!" She fanned herself as warmth spread across her cheeks.

"Look around, my dear. We are anything but alone."

The bailey was teeming with guests from the castle, vendors, gypsies, and villagers.

"You look tired. Would you like to retire for a few hours before the feast begins this afternoon? Remember there is a dance too. Christmas celebrations in the castle are usually lots of fun. I left strict instructions with my staff to ensure the Wallingford residents properly celebrated even in my absence."

"Yes, Grey. I am suddenly tired. More emotionally spent than physically tired. I definitely need some rest before putting on my dancing slippers. I have learned a lot today. About me. About Oliver and Stephen. And mostly, about you."

"I hope all of it brings you pleasure."

"Most of it, yes. We have a lot of talking to do before you will know if you truly want me to be the mother of your children. After we are through, you may want to look elsewhere for the next Duchess of Wallingford. Remember, the gypsy said we needed total truth between us. There are things you do not know about me." She smiled weakly.

Grey bent down and kissed her cheek. "It seems unlikely I will throw you over for Lady Cecelia. No matter what news you have to impart. Let us go back to the keep."

****

Maisie helped Emmeline out of her dress. She crawled under the covers in her chemise but no matter how long she kept her eyes closed, she could not sleep. She got out of bed, put on her dressing gown and slippers, and curled up in the chair in front of the fire with a soft woolen blanket around her shoulders and another across her lap.

She was still there when Eleanor came rushing into the room thirty minutes later. "Oh, good. You are here, Emmie. What a morning I have had."

"Exciting mornings must run in the family today. Tell me about yours before Maisie comes back to ready us for the feast and dance."

"We spent an extra long time drinking tea in the breakfast room. By we, I mean Simon and me. We were the last ones remaining at the table before we were shooed out. Simon spent most of the time telling me about his estate, Summerton. It is located in-between here and our home. Almost exactly halfway. You know he is an only child. The house and grounds sound divine. His parents are a little older than ours were. He said he was a surprise child much to his mother's embarrassment.

"When they chased us out of the keep we went to enjoy the carnival. The carousel, the side shows, and, of course, some of the wonderful sweets. You know I can never resist a well-made tart. We were in the crowd when little Oliver won the donkey race. How exciting."

"Sounds like you did a lot of the same things I did this morning with Grey and his nephews."

"Probably, what fun…wait…Grey? You mean His Grace?"

"No, I mean Grey. He asked me to call him by his first name and he is calling me Eleanor, not Miss Eleanor or Miss Brown. I only agreed to call him Grey when no one else is around."

"Oh, Emmie, that is wonderful. Simon calls me Emmeline. I am getting used to it and almost beginning to believe I am you. He asked when my father would be here because he has something important to discuss with him."

"Congratulations, Ellie. I told you that you would not need to look for a governess position next year. You will be busy preparing to be a viscountess. Grey and I went to the Romany fortune teller. She said we were going to marry one another and have a forever love— once there is total truth between us. Grey is referring to me as the future mother of his children."

"How perfect. Your father and Aunt Clementine will be so excited when they get here. We will both have husbands soon."

"Stop and think for a minute, Ellie. Grey did not ask to speak with my father because he believes I am the orphaned Miss Brown. What have we gotten into?" Emmie shook her head.

"We are in the perfect place. You wanted proof a suitor loved you and not your money. The duke has no idea you have a dowry. He loves you and wants you to have his children even though he needs money for his estate. My goodness, it does not get more romantic than that."

"But the cat will be out of the bag once Papa arrives and Simon asks for the hand of Lady Emmeline Spenser."

"No. I think we have to let it play out until formal proposals have been made. Your father will be the one to give permission for me to be married as well."

"We have to find a way to end this ruse before they make their formal proposals. I do not want to start life with Grey on a lie. It would be a very bad beginning. And I do not want him to think he has chosen love at the expense of his estate. There must be a way to work it out."

"Perhaps we should pray for a little Divine intervention. Maybe if we tell Aunt Clementine what we have done, she can help us find a solution."

"Both are excellent suggestions. Auntie with Divine back up will be unstoppable."

The cousins hugged.

****

Grey rapped lightly on the door then stuck his head into his sister's sitting room. "Have you got a minute, Caro?"

"Of course. You look troubled." Caroline moved from the desk to the settee and patted the cushion beside her. "Sit."

"I can deny it no longer. Eleanor Brown is going to be the next Duchess of Wallingford. The Romany fortune teller said we would have a long and happy life together with daring sons and sweet daughters."

"You are selecting your future bride based on gypsy recommendations?"

"No. I had started thinking about it long before the seer outlined our future. It is your fault. You decided I needed to marry. I believe you are right. She has a sweet side and an unexpectedly sassy one. She is neither a submissive wall flower nor a grasping title seeker. She is simply Eleanor. I did not think it was possible but she is everything I want in a wife without even knowing I was seriously looking."

"My, you are smitten. So the problem is one of dowry?"

"She has none."

"It may not be so bleak. Perhaps Lord Crestmont will settle some token dowry on her as her guardian. Or perhaps her parents provided for her prior to their untimely deaths."

"She believes she has none. It is a problem I need to resolve. The gypsy said we needed total truth between us for our love to thrive. I have to tell her about my estate's financial condition before I ask her to be my bride. I am not sure how to proceed."

"Have you talked to our godfather?"

"No, I have not. It is an excellent idea. Wingate may be able to help me find a solution. I told Richard I wanted the kind of marriage you and he have, not a business arrangement for heir creation. I should have been more specific in what I wished for."

Caroline leaned over and kissed his cheek. "Au contraire, mon frère. I believe it will all work out swimmingly well. Have a little faith in the lady and in yourself. I am glad you decided on love. I want my brother to be as happy as I am."

Grey kissed her cheek and left.

"My determined bachelor brother has fallen hard. I

hope our godfather has something to help," she said aloud.

****

Maisie curled their hair, used ribbon as a headband, and left it loose on their shoulders for tonight's festivities.

Emmeline wore an emerald-green gown with a gold bodice. Eleanor's frock was sapphire blue with a gold bodice. Their necklines curved gracefully and modestly, revealing no cleavage. Both dresses had sleeves ending in gold tips to match their bodices. The crinolines beneath the skirts made them full. They rustled with a swish of silk when they walked. Their dancing slippers were black with gold buckles.

The massive pale gray stone Great Hall of the castle was adorned in pine boughs, holly branches, and mistletoe. The scent of pine and roasting meats permeated the air. Long tables laden with food were at the short ends of the hall. The tall Christmas tree they had decorated earlier glistened with sparkling ornaments and candles at one side of the room. Tables and benches for people to eat at filled the hall.

The centerpiece of each food table was a massive roast hog with an apple in its mouth. The hide was peeled back to reveal succulent pork that had been cooking in the ground for three days. Golden brown roasted geese and juicy swans were cut into pieces for easy eating. A huge roast beef spun on the pit over the gigantic stone fireplace at each end of the hall. Staff were there to cut off whatever amount the guests desired. There were orange roasted yams and brown potatoes arranged on platters. Caldrons full of bubbling leek and potato soup rested by the fire. Fresh baked bread, delicate tarts, berry laden muffins, iced cakes, and delicious fruit-filled pies weighed down one end of the buffet. Vats of mead and pitchers of ale were available to quench the party goers' thirsts.

When the Earl and Countess Chelmsford declared the feast open, revelers poured through the doors. Everyone had on their very best clothes and manners. The Romany men and women wore costumes with flashing gold and silver medallions hanging from them. The village children looked well-scrubbed and were wide-eyed at the array of food before them.

The revelers filled their plates and took in the festive environment in the room. Lord and Lady Chelmsford walked among the feasters kissing children and hugging long-time staff. They encouraged everyone to go back to fill their plates again and to keep eating until their stomachs were full.

When the feasting was over, everyone helped to stack the tables on the side of the room and line the benches along the perimeter of the hall to clear space in the middle for dancing. The musicians came in and set up on the balcony at the top of the stairs so music floated down from on high.

The Romany took the floor in a whirl of color, jangling of bracelets, and clapping to the music. The staccato clicking of their heels on the stone floor sped up as the tempo of the music increased. Everyone was mesmerized by the exhibition of passion and rhythm. When they finished, the audience was almost as breathless as the Romany were.

Lord and Lady Chelmsford led off the first dance for all the guests, a lively reel. Not quite at the furious tempo of the gypsy dancers, but fast enough to get everyone's blood flowing and lungs panting for breath. Everyone danced, regardless of age. Whether you lived in the castle or a cottage, you were expected to participate in the revelry.

The castle guests danced exclusively with one another to begin with. Then some of the young men of the village challenged one another to invite one of the fine ladies to the dance floor. Lady Emmeline and Miss Brown were the first guests to accept their invitations. Even the Dowager Countess Chelmsford enjoyed a few dances with old friends. Many of her dance partners also danced with Lady Crowley, remembering her visits to her sister in years earlier. After the ice had been broken, the lords began inviting the women of the village to dance.

Emmeline and Eleanor hadn't sat down. They were in high demand as dance partners by young and old men from both the castle and the cottages. It was uninhibited, rollicking fun. All of the guests seemed to be enjoying the festivities except Lady Cecelia who sat off to the side scowling at anyone who dared to ask her to dance. Her eyes were glued on the duke who was making the rounds of the cottagers. Lord Edward asked her for a waltz and she finally consented though her eyes continued to follow the duke.

The cousins were standing together after an especially taxing number. "Oh, my, I am not sure I could dance one more step. I am having such fun but my legs are so tired. I am afraid to sit down for fear I shall never be able to stand again. I am definitely done dancing for the evening."

"I am sorry to hear that, Miss Brown," a deep, familiar voice said. The duke bowed. "I was about to ask you to join me on the floor. If you are too fatigued I shall ask your cousin if she will consent to the next dance."

Lord Simon appeared at 'Emmeline's' side. "Apologies, Your Grace, but this lady has promised me all the dances for the rest of the evening." The music began and he swept his Lady Emmeline onto the floor.

'Eleanor' laughed. "Looks like you are stuck with the tired vicar's daughter. I believe I am revived sufficiently for this waltz, Your Grace."

The duke pulled her into his strong arms and onto the dance floor. Her knees wobbled when he touched the small of her back. Her stomach did flip-flops in time with the music. She nestled against his chest breathing in his unique, very masculine scent. He was easy to dance with. The subtle pressure on her back kept her in perfect step with him. Did he truly want her to be the mother of his children? His duchess? The music stopped and Grey still held her.

"May I interest you in another?" Grey whispered in her ear. It felt like she belonged here next to his heart, under his protection, for the rest of his life. He was more certain than ever that Eleanor Brown was destined to be his bride. Love weighed more than dowry.

"Absolutely," she whispered.

He began gliding across the floor with her snug against his chest.

"I am glad to see you recover quickly. I believe I mentioned my estate, Wallingford, has a similar celebration to this one each year. My people will be delighted when I bring home a dancing duchess." His eyes glistened with adoration.

"Your Grace, I would be more than honored to

dance with you at Wallingford."

"Please do not misunderstand. I intend to speak with your guardian, if you consent. Is it Lord Crestmont? Lady Emmeline's father?"

"Yes. But I should like to discuss this proposal with you before you speak with him. You are making a marriage proposal, correct?"

"Yes. I am. And I know about your dowry situation. No further discussion is needed."

"Forgive me, Grey, but there are some details about marrying the woman you are holding in your arms that you are unaware of. Lord Crestmont will be here the day after Christmas. I am sure we shall find time to talk before then."

"As I have noted before, you are a bit cheeky, my dear."

She gasped.

"But I have always liked a little sass in my women." He laughed and hugged her tighter.

"Your women? It sounds like you have some details about your past to share with me as well, Your Grace."

The music stopped. Lord Edward stepped to the duke's side. He said, "Wallingford, old man, Cece, Lady Cecelia, has been dying to dance with you. It would make my life much more congenial if you would exchange partners with me for the next dance."

Grey laughed. "Consider it done. I hope you do not mind, Miss Brown."

"Of course not, Your Grace."

The music resumed. It was a lively reel. Lord Edward led 'Eleanor' to the floor and the duke led an unsmiling Lady Cecelia out. After the last note ended, she grabbed the duke's arm.

"For a woman who was supposedly dying to dance with me, you do not look too happy," Grey noted when the music stopped.

"Your Grace, I was hoping for something where you would take me in your arms, not a steeplechase on the dance floor. Would you dance the next one with me too?" Cecelia asked.

The duke bowed. "I apologize Lady Cecelia. I have promised this one to Miss Brown." He turned and walked to the edge of the floor leaving her gaping and glaring after him until Lord Edward took her in his arms for the waltz that was playing.

The duke swept his Miss Brown onto the dance floor. She smelled like roses, like the ones he loved to grow. He had told Richard he did not want a broodmare. It was true, but he would love to have a houseful of children with Eleanor. Beautiful children with his black eyes and her chestnut hair. He wanted love. The real thing. Her love. He appeared to have gotten it.

What could possibly be worrying Eleanor about a future with him? Had she heard about his financial problems? Was she worried he would not be able to support her? She was only a vicar's daughter, but she had been raised as if she was Lady Emmeline Spenser's sister. He needed to have answers for her when they talked. And for her guardian. No one wanted to send their favorite niece into matrimony with a man who had a dicey financial future. Not even with a duke.

"Darling, the music has stopped. That was the last song," she said softly.

Grey dropped his arms. "Sorry, deep in thought."

"Rethinking your earlier offer?"

"Never."

Lady Chelmsford sent the villagers home with bundles filled with leftovers for them to enjoy on Christmas day. Each child received an apple and some candy-coated almonds. Delight glowed on each and every face.

Chapter Ten

Emmeline woke early Christmas Eve morning. She was still exhausted and excited from all of yesterday's events. She went to the window and cracked it open. A blanket of glistening white snow covered the bailey and the woods and hills beyond it making everything look clean, pure, and bright. It wasn't too deep. Just enough to make a perfect Christmas picture.

All the tents were coming down and vardos being packed as the vendors and Romany prepared for a move farther south. There would be more carnivals for them as they sought warmer weather. The zebra, elephant, and camel looked confused about the white stuff under their feet. Emmie could hear the monkey chattering all the way from her window. She couldn't help but smile thinking of Stephen and Lady Cecelia. Out of the mouths of babes.

A man from the castle strode across the bailey in hat and cape. He crossed the moat on the snow-covered drawbridge and headed directly to one of the Romany vardos. What was he doing? Emmeline watched him talking with one of the gypsy craftsmen. He paid the man. Moments later the Rom came from the brightly colored wagon with something wrapped in a colorful piece of fabric. The man tipped his hat and headed back to the keep at a brisk walk. She leaned out the window to get a better look. It was Grey. Who was he buying something for out in the snow so early this morning? Chilled, she retreated back into the room, closed the window, and nestled in front of the fire until Ellie stirred.

****

Grey knocked the snow off his boots inside the front door in the entrance hall. It was early but his godfather had always been one to rise with the sun. He took the stair steps two at a time to the second floor. Caro said Wingate was in the first room at the top of the stairs. He knocked. The duke's man, Chesterton, answered.

"Good morning, Chesterton. Is His Grace available to see his only godson this morning?"

Chesterton bowed slightly. "Good to see you, Your Grace. He is having a little tea by the fire. May I bring you a cup?"

"Perfect. Thank you."

Grey walked into the sitting room. His godfather stood to greet him.

"Please do not get up. I need a few minutes of your time and advice on an important matter."

"Come in, my boy. I was quite certain I would be seeing you this morning."

"You were? I did not know I needed to see you until late last night."

"That is the thing about love. By the time you realize you are unable to live without her, you are almost the last to recognize your condition." The older duke laughed.

"Am I so obvious?"

"In a word, yes. She is a perfectly lovely girl. You seemed well suited on the dance floor. She shows the same sometimes fiery spirit your mother did as a young woman. But is she not nearly identical to her well-dowered cousin, Lady Emmeline Spenser?"

"In looks perhaps, but they have completely different personalities. Eleanor Brown is the one I love. Even with no dowry. It is part of what I have come to discuss with you. The Earl of Crestmont, her uncle, is her guardian. I am concerned I may not be exactly who he envisioned his niece would marry. Financially. You know Thomas left the estate finances in shambles. I need to be in a position to assure Crestmont I can provide for Eleanor in the manner she is accustomed to. He thinks of her as another daughter."

"Has the young lady expressed a concern about your income or financial stability?"

"No, but she told me we needed to discuss our relationship in more detail before I speak with her guardian. I can think of no other concern she could have."

"Because you have told her you love her? And she has told you the same?"

"Not in those exact words. I told her I wanted her to be the mother of my children and to dance with her as the Duchess of Wallingford. Is it not the same thing?"

"I am afraid not, my boy. Women are strange creatures when it comes to hearing those very specific words, unless they are title hunting witches of Lady Cecelia Thompson's ilk. Her type does not care about the love part of the equation although I do believe she expects there to be a substantial income to go with the title. There are no words any woman believes are equivalent to the three little words—I love you."

Grey shook his head. "You know all about Lady Cecelia by watching her from afar. You are a wise man. I need to tell Eleanor I love her immediately then because, God help me, I do, with all my heart. What can I do about replacing her dowry?"

"Chesterton," Duke Wingate called. "Please bring me the satchel with Wallingford's papers. Thank you."

"Wallingford's papers? What do you have for me?"

"Toward the end of his life, your father became concerned about your brother's ability to manage and sustain the estate long term. Your father loved the people of Wallingford and felt a great responsibility for their wellbeing. You inherited his views. Your brother did not feel the need to maintain his legacy in the same way. Six months before your father died, he and your mother came to me with the lion's share of your mother's fine jewelry. Part of it had been her dowry. A number of her pieces were in Caroline's dowry. They asked me to hold the satchel and its contents until and unless it was needed for the survival of Wallingford and its residents. Your father feared giving Thomas the estate, the money, and the jewelry simultaneously would simply encourage his wastrel behavior. Your mother wanted the next Duchess of Wallingford to have her jewelry, not one of your brother's doxies. I still have the jewelry." Chesterton handed his master the requested satchel. "It includes your mother's emerald wedding ring which came to me on her passing. I am giving you this bequest on behalf of your parents. You need it now."

Grey's hands trembled as he reached for the treasures. "I cannot believe you did not give it to Thomas. He was certainly running short of funds at the end."

"I am not sure why I hesitated. I am simply thankful that I did. Otherwise, these too would be gone and you and your duchess would be in a financial bind. Not to mention the people of your estate."

Grey spread the pieces of jewelry on the table in front of him. "I am speechless. I was going to ask Caroline what had become of mother's emerald ring. It matches Eleanor's green eyes exactly. Now I have the financial means to tell her I love her. I am much more confident Lord Crestmont will approve of our marriage. This bequest makes all things possible. Eleanor cannot hesitate now. Thank you for helping my parents and, more, for coming to my aid at this moment of greatest need. I cannot believe you thought to bring the satchel with you to Winterhaven."

"You can thank your sweet sister for that bit of providence. She told me in my invitation that it was her intention to find you a wife before the new year. I thought the satchel would be needed or at least the wedding ring would. Your sister is an unstoppable force when her mind is set on a particular objective."

"That is a dramatic understatement. She told me her goal shortly after I arrived. I was foolish enough to laugh in her face. I am glad she warned you. Everything seems to be working toward a new year's marriage. I cannot believe it, but I am actually delighted with the prospect. Thank you again. I need to go and find my soon-to-be-bride."

Grey stood, shook hands, then hugged his godfather, and took the satchel. He bumped into Lady Cecelia as he came out of the room.

"Pardon me," he said hurriedly and went down the

stairs quickly.

"This must be the duke's room." She stood back and counted the number of doors down the hall to the right—four, and to the left—three. She had a plan for how to proceed. Cecelia cackled. "He will have to do the right thing now."

****

Grey left the satchel with Jackson to secure in the bottom of his trunk. He found 'Eleanor' and her cousin in the breakfast room conversing over coffee with his sister.

"Good morning, ladies. Did you see we have snow for Christmas? It is a winter wonderland outside," Grey announced cheerfully. He walked to the end of the table and kissed his sister on the cheek. "Do we have a sleigh?"

"Yes. Actually two four-seaters. Thinking a Christmas Eve sleigh ride is in order?" Caroline asked.

"What do you ladies think? Would you like to go?" Grey nodded to Emmeline and Eleanor.

"Sounds like great fun," his Eleanor responded.

Lord Simon came in the room. "Whatever it is, count me in. I am always up for great fun!"

His Emmeline said, "A sleigh ride."

"Sounds delightful," Simon replied.

"One sleigh full is ready!" Grey announced.

Lady Beatrice, Lord William, Lord Edward, and Lady Cornelia quickly filled the second sleigh. As the group had almost reached the stable, Oliver and Stephen came running across the bailey.

"Uncle Grey! Uncle Grey! Please take us along with you. We want to go on a sleigh ride too."

"They are small," his Eleanor said. "One can sit

with Emmie and one with us, Grey."

"I cannot tell them no, even though it will not quite be the romantic ride I had envisioned."

"I knew you would not deny them. It is Christmas snow. Nothing is more special than that. It will be romantic. I shall be next to you."

"You mean practically next to me?" he said as Stephen plopped down between them on the seat.

Lady Cecelia arrived in the courtyard as the second sleigh crossed the drawbridge into the meadow beyond. "The nerve of him going without me. At least they are well chaperoned with those little tykes along on the ride. Soon it will be impossible for the Duke of Wallingford to ignore me. Very soon."

Lady Chelmsford had hearty bowls of vegetable soup and cups of cocoa waiting for luncheon when the revelers returned. All were rosy cheeked and smiling. Especially her sons. Uncle Grey had let them each take a turn driving the team through the snow.

After lunch, Grey asked his intended if she would like to go for a bracing stroll outside. She agreed. They were in the snow-covered garden when two little boys raced out of the keep.

"Uncle Grey! Mother said we could build a snowman as long as we did not get out of your sight. Will you help us?" Oliver asked.

"Look, we have everything we need for him," Stephen added.

"Let us see. A top hat. A scarf. Two lumps of coal for his eyes. A carrot for his nose. Holly berries for his mouth," 'Eleanor' went through the inventory. "I think you have it all covered. C'mon, Uncle Grey. It will be lots of fun."

"My sister seems determined to keep us from being alone," Grey muttered.

She grabbed his hand. "Come on. I have never built a snowman with a duke before." She smiled and winked.

They gathered every bit of snow in and around the garden into three well-packed balls. The boys set the middle sized one on the large one. 'Miss Eleanor' helped them create the face on the smallest ball. Uncle Grey balanced it on top of the other two, crowned it with a hat, and wrapped the scarf around its neck.

"Ta-da!" Oliver said.

"Oh, no. He has no arms," Stephen said. They ran to a corner of the garden where some small branches had come down in the snow.

Grey reached for 'Eleanor's' hand. "When my nephews allow us some private time together, I have wonderful news to share with you. You should have no financial worries about marrying me."

"We need to talk also for you to be certain there are no concerns about me becoming the next Duchess of Wallingford."

Their brief discussion ended when the boys brought over the perfect branches for the snowman's arms. The snowman builders were all cold with wet and soggy clothes when they returned to the keep.

Cook gave them mugs full of cocoa in the kitchen by a roaring fire. Grey wanted to go to the library to talk but 'Eleanor' protested she needed to rest before the Christmas Eve festivities started at tea time.

Her cousin was in their room napping when Emmeline returned. Maisie helped her out of her wet clothes in front of the recently replenished fire. She curled up in a blanket in the chair and watched the flames shoot blue, yellow, and red strings of color into the fireplace. She was exhausted but she couldn't think about sleeping. Tears seeped out of her eyes and dripped down her cheeks.

This whole situation had rapidly gotten out of hand. She had to tell Grey the truth now. It couldn't wait until Papa and Aunt Clementine arrived. Would he want to marry her after he knew she had been masquerading as her cousin? Could he ever understand her reasons? They had dreamed up the scheme before she'd ever met him. Everyone knows heiresses are at risk of being duped into loveless marriages just to get at their money. If Grey were a lesser man, he might even have done it given his situation.

Ellie got out of bed, stretched, and wandered over to the chair her cousin was in. "Scoot over. Make room for me." She crawled under the blanket. "You look upset. Have you been crying?"

"Oh, Ellie, I love him so much. We have to tell Simon and Grey the truth. The sooner the better. I do not want to wait for Papa to arrive. I feel like I shall explode if I do not tell him soon."

"I am glad to hear you say you are ready. I almost blurted it out to Simon today coming back in the sleigh when the boys were both in the front seat with you and the duke. This evening will be impossible. We would be missed. Perhaps tomorrow morning after Christmas services in the chapel. The four of us could go somewhere alone. They need to hear it at the same time."

"And, more importantly, you and I need to be together for moral support."

"Agreed."

****

After tea, everyone gathered around the Christmas tree in the Great Hall. Lord Chelmsford began pulling small gifts off the branches and distributing them to his family and guests. Everyone had at least one gift to unwrap. Oliver and Stephen garnered the most being the only children present.

'Emmeline' received a small gift from Simon. She opened it to find a Romany-crafted delicate gold filigree broach with a small emerald at the center of it. She had worked in her room in spare moments and made him a fine linen handkerchief and embroidered his initials on it.

'Eleanor' was surprised when Grey gave her a gift wrapped in bright-colored fabric. The same bundle she'd seen him bring across the bailey earlier that morning. She carefully unwrapped it to find a blown glass rose—the one she'd admired during their walk through the Romany vardos and carnival grounds. She had borrowed yarn and knitting needles from Lady Chelmsford and knit Grey an elegant scarf. He teased her about having time to knit when she had all those books she'd borrowed from the library she needed to read. She cuffed him playfully.

The boys ran around the tree gathering up the brightly colored tubes tied with a ribbon on each end—the crackers. They were passed out and each couple worked together to pull them open. Soon the popping sound of successful openings filled the air. The poems and candies were for the women and the men were each crowned with a silly paper hat. Lady Margaret and His Grace the Duke of Wingate shared a cracker; Beatrice and William; Cornelia and Paul; Lord and Lady Bollingwood; Lord and Lady Castleberry; Lord Richard and Lady Chelmsford; Edward and Cecelia; Grey and 'Eleanor'; and Simon and 'Emmeline'. The boys each got one and split one with Nanny and one with Lady Crowley. The ladies got the poems. The boys donned the paper hats and shared the sugary treats too.

As people were going to the dining room, Lady Cecelia pulled on Grey's arm. "I have a gift for you, Your Grace."

She waved to Lord Edward to leave her there. He stopped at the edge of the room and offered his arm to 'Eleanor' who stood glaring at Cecelia. After Grey nodded, 'Eleanor' went with Edward to the dining room.

"Lady Cecelia, I am surprised. I have no gift for you. I must decline your generosity."

She stomped her foot like a child having a temper tantrum. "Why can you take *her* gift and not mine?"

"The circumstances between Miss Brown and myself are totally different than those between you and I. Please, do not embarrass yourself or me further by insisting I accept your gift."

Grey left her standing in the Great Hall holding a silver wrapped package. She threw it down under the tree and joined Edward in the dining room. Unfortunately, to sit next to 'Eleanor', Cecelia was on his other side.

Dinner was a feast of creamy butternut squash soup with a dusting of nutmeg on top; crisp skinned roast goose with delicious chestnut stuffing; and an assortment of roasted vegetables from the root cellar. The wonderful feast was topped off with flaming plum pudding covered with Cook's special rum sauce. Everyone groaned from overeating by the end of the meal.

After dinner, Grey led the entire group to the hothouse so Caroline could receive her Christmas gift from him. With great flourish, he took down the curtain blocking the corner and revealed the elegant, sweet-smelling, four-color, Lady Caroline Winter Rose. His twin burst into tears.

"You never cease to amaze me, sweet brother. Thank you."

"Why are you crying, Mother? Are you not happy? Do you not like Uncle Grey's present?" Stephen asked.

"Sometimes tears are good. When you are so excited and happy that they have to pop out. That is how I feel right now. I love Uncle Grey's gift," their mother explained.

"It is another complicated woman thing," Oliver said. "Maybe we shall understand when we are older."

Chapter Eleven

The bells in the small chapel located in the back corner of the bailey rang out announcing the arrival of Christmas morning. The cousins walked together into the intimate sanctuary and entered a pew near the front behind the Winter family. Other guests filed in quietly.

The vicar's message was one of hope and rejoicing. The music made Emmeline's heart soar. She sat almost directly behind Grey. His rich baritone voice gave her shivers as they sang "Hark, the Herald Angels Sing."

Emmeline waited outside the chapel to speak with Grey. Lady Caroline stopped to talk with her first.

"Good morning. I wanted to let you know we are expecting more guests today. Your aunt sent me a note saying she and your uncle were going to try to come today instead of tomorrow. I hope they do. It would be a shame for them to miss the Christmas ball. We have neighbors from estates within two days drive coming in today too. There will be no room at this inn by midnight tonight." She laughed.

"Sounds like an exciting celebration." Emmeline turned to Eleanor. "Papa, your papa, may be in tonight for the ball with Aunt Clementine."

"Then there is no time to lose," Eleanor said. She pointed to the duke coming out of the chapel.

"Excuse us, please. Your Grace, could I speak to you a moment?" Emmeline asked Grey.

They huddled together briefly.

"I understand. Perhaps there will be time when you return."

The cousins went to their room.

"The men are going hunting," Emmeline announced. "They are looking for deer, geese, pheasants, rabbits, and quail. Grey said they hoped to replenish Lord Chelmsford's larder that we have been enjoying all week."

"What a kind thing to do. Very much in the Christmas spirit," Eleanor said. "But it runs afoul of our plan to enlighten the gentlemen on our identities before your papa arrives."

"Yes, it does. But it might be a good thing. If Papa will be here today, we can alert Aunt Clementine to the situation so she can help."

At lunch time, the hunters had not yet returned. Oliver and Stephen joined their mother and the female guests for a little something to eat. They regaled the guests with tales of the new snow-white foal and a new white kid they had named Sugar, born to their angora goat.

After they had eaten, Emmeline asked, "Do you boys know how to get in the tower room? I have been curious about it ever since we arrived."

"Yes, Miss Eleanor, we do. But Mother never lets us go alone. We could invite Perry to go with us," Oliver said.

"An excellent idea, Oliver. Perry, would you accompany these ladies and young lads up to the south tower room? From there you will be able to watch coaches coming to the castle in one direction and possibly spy our hunting party in the woods," Lady

Chelmsford said.

Oliver and Stephen led the way. Then Emmeline, Eleanor, Beatrice, and Cornelia. Cecelia declined the offer saying the tower was probably full of cobwebs and other disgusting things. Perry, the footman, brought up the rear. The narrow steps were quite steep. They only allowed for single file passage and seemed to go on forever. When they reached the top, Stephen announced, "We are here."

They crowded into the small hall at the top of the stairs outside a heavy oaken door leading to the tower room. Perry lifted the bar holding it shut and pulled on the large metal ring to open it. The door groaned in protest. When it was ajar enough for the boys to scoot through the opening, they entered the room and pushed from the other side to help Perry get the door fully open.

A blast of cold air rearranged Emmeline's curls. "Goodness, the weather is much colder up here," she said.

"It is but the view is worth it," Lady Beatrice said.

The ladies stepped to the windows. Oliver and Stephen pointed out landmarks across the estate from their high vantage point. Two carriages were coming down the road in the distance. Eleanor spotted horsemen in the woods and rifle shots rang through the air.

"The hunters must have found something," Lady Cornelia said. "Nothing is quite as good as fresh venison roast."

"I hope they hit the mark," Eleanor said.

Perry stepped forward saying, "Ladies, I do not mean to rush anyone. You are welcome to stay as long as you would like. However, the temperature seems to be dropping and I would recommend we make our way back down the stairs and into the main keep before it gets much colder."

Everyone agreed with Perry. Oliver and Stephen helped the footman close the door and secure it with the bar as the ladies started their descent.

****

Clementine looked out the window of the coach. "I can see Winterhaven from here. It seems enchanted the way the gray stones glisten with frost. No wonder Caroline loves it here."

"I hope our girls have been having a good stay," Lord Crestmont said. "Emmeline was adamant she was not going to husband hunt while she was here. I hope her views on becoming a wife have softened a little. I am relieved she wanted Eleanor to accompany her. Her cousin always seems to know the perfect thing to say for Emmeline to reconsider her strongly held opinions."

"Watching the two of them together reminds me of growing up with their mothers. Since I was four years older, the twins wanted nothing to do with me. They lived in their own little world. Emmeline and Eleanor look like one another but like Amelia and Cordelia too. I wish they could see their beautiful daughters now. Poor Papa kept wanting a son and instead got a trio of girls."

"I am glad he had three beautiful daughters. Thank you, Clemmie, for being here to help your nieces. They both love you so much." He kissed her hand. "Almost as much as I do."

"What do you think they will say about us? Will they be upset? Should we have waited to tie the knot until we told them we planned to wed?"

"That ship has sailed, my love. This was the perfect time to get away together. Besides, with any luck, they will be so besotted with romances of their own they will hardly take notice of ours. My Emmeline has always wanted me to be happy and she has been worried about me being alone. I think that has been part of her reluctance to marry and leave home. Now, we have removed that impediment to her happiness. I am so proud to have you at my side. Forever. I know Amelia is too." He leaned over and kissed her cheek.

She reddened. "You make me blush like a schoolgirl. I am not accustomed to such flowery words and displays of affection."

"You need to get used to them. Charles did not know what he had or how much love you had to give. He was a fool. I am not."

"I am so thankful. You know I could not love Emmeline and Eleanor more if I had birthed them myself."

"They know it, Clemmie. They have the greatest affection for you."

The drawbridge groaned as the coach rolled over it and clattered onto the cobblestones leading to the keep's front door.

"We are here," Lord Crestmont said.

A group of women came out of the south tower followed by two young boys and a footman.

"Yoo hoo!" Clementine called as she stepped out of the coach. "Emmeline and Eleanor."

The cousins waved back and started toward the couple descending from the coach they had seen from the tower. They fell upon the newly arrived guests with hugs and kisses.

"Papa. Aunt Clementine."

"Uncle. Aunt Clementine."

Moments later, Lady Caroline came out to greet her guests. "My dear Clementine. I am so glad you changed your plans to be here for the Christmas ball tonight. It is a wonderful gift for your nieces." She kissed Clementine's cheek.

"Caroline, I cannot thank you enough for the hospitality you have extended to my nieces. This is Lord Randolph Spenser, the Earl of Crestmont. He is Emmeline's father and Eleanor's uncle and guardian."

"Pleased to meet you. Let us go inside where it is warmer. I hope your accommodations will be acceptable. I have given you one of our suites with two bedrooms and a sitting room between them. We are going to have a full house this evening."

"It will be perfect, Lady Chelmsford," Lord Crestmont said with a twinkle in his eye.

Clementine blushed and followed their hostess into the keep and up the broad stone stairs to their suite. The girls came close behind them, pointing out their room as they passed it.

Before Caroline left she whispered to Clementine, "I think you will find your nieces had a wonderful week. I shall not be surprised to be hosting some New Year's Eve weddings. We shall see you at tea time in the gold salon. I shall leave you to get settled in."

"Clementine, I am going to my room to rest a bit. Traveling takes more out of me than it used to. The girls seem anxious to talk to you." Lord Crestmont kissed all three of them and crossed the sitting room.

Emmeline began as soon as her father was out of

the room, "Oh, Auntie, we desperately need your advice."

"We have gotten into a bit of a mess," Eleanor said.

"A mess? Lady Caroline implied you had good news for us, not a problem."

"We do, but we have some unraveling to do to get to the happy part," Emmeline said.

The cousins explained the plan they'd hatched to ensure Emmeline found a husband who loved her, not one who loved her money. Clementine listened quietly asking clarifying questions from time to time. They talked about long horseback rides, picnics, and a carnival with Romany fortune tellers. They even told her about jealous Lady Cecelia Thompson. A sly smile crossed the aunt's face.

"So, the dilemma is that Lord Summerly is going to ask for Lady Emmeline's hand in marriage, but he has actually fallen in love with Eleanor. And the Duke of Wallingford is going to ask for Eleanor's hand, but he is really in love with Emmeline. Right?"

"Exactly," the cousins said in unison.

"And the jig will be up when Papa straightens them out. We should have told the gentlemen before now, but it all flipped from like to love to marriage proposals rather quickly. For both of us," Emmeline said. "How can we tell them our true identities before they try to talk with Papa?"

"And then there is the dowry problem. Simon says it does not matter. What if it does and he is only saying that because he thinks I have one?" Eleanor said blinking back tears.

"Do you trust me to work this out?" Clementine

asked.

"Yes!"

"Lady Caroline must have an inkling about all of this or she would not have told me you had good news. I may have to enlist her assistance. Do I have your permission?"

Emmeline hesitated. "Her brother is the duke I am in love with."

"I know."

"Yes, I guess you will find the best way to handle it."

"Then go and get some rest before tea. I certainly need some."

Clementine shooed them from the sitting room. Randolph came out of his room and walked over to her side. He pulled her into an embrace and a long kiss.

"I hope you are not too exhausted, my lady wife."

"You are incorrigible."

"Did you share our news with the girls?"

"No. They have a problem they need my help to solve. Indirectly it involves you. If I share the dilemma with you, sweet husband, you must promise to follow my lead on this and act totally surprised when the gentlemen in question ask to speak with you. Do you swear to abide by these rules?"

He crossed his heart. "I do."

Clementine explained the situation and how she proposed to resolve it.

He began laughing. "I guess I have no objection to the girls having a secret when we have a whopper to reveal to them. Sounds like you have this issue well in hand. I defer to your expertise in matters of the heart."

****

The hunting party returned in mid-afternoon well pleased with the results of their expedition. They had a dozen hares, four brace of pheasants, six large geese, two large stags, and even a fat black bear. Enough to keep the Winterhaven huntsmen and kitchen staff quite busy dressing out the fresh meat for several days.

The duke stopped and rapped on their bedroom door as he passed. Maisie answered and said, "His Grace is in the hall and would like to speak to you, Miss Eleanor."

Emmeline waited until Maisie returned to the alcove at the back of their room where she was doing some last-minute alterations on one of their gowns for this evening's ball. Emmeline stepped to the door.

"Please come in. Emmeline is here as well."

"No, I do not want to set tongues to wagging. I just got in and desperately need to wash and change before tea time. Do we still need to talk before then?"

"No. It can wait until later this evening. Lord Crestmont and our aunt, Lady Guilderswood, arrived while you were out so you will meet them at tea."

"I look forward to it. See you soon." He bowed slightly and continued down the hall.

She closed the door. "I hope Auntie has a great plan for how to straighten all this out."

"I pray she does," Ellie added.

Chapter Twelve

Lady Guilderwood and Lady Chelmsford were in deep conversation sitting side-by-side on a settee. Lord Chelmsford and Lord Crestmont were both smoking pipes standing by the fireplace discussing the day's hunting expedition. Gradually, the salon filled with the guests who had been there all week and the new arrivals. Lady Chelmsford made introductions as new people came into the room. She asked Lady Cecelia if she would do the honor of pouring for the party. Lady Cecelia protested briefly, then happily assumed the hostess's duty clearly relishing being the chosen one.

The duke came into the room after Cecelia had already poured for everyone else.

"Your Grace, I was beginning to wonder what had happened to you. How would you like your tea?"

"Exactly like Lady Chelmsford's," he said with a smile.

"I am sorry, I have poured so many cups I do not recall how your sister takes her tea." Splotches of red covered her cheeks.

"Your Grace, do not be such a wicked creature. He wants it with a spot of cream and a dash of honey."

"Thank you, Lady Chelmsford." Cecelia poured the duke's tea and handed it to him with trembling hands.

"Thank you. Sorry for being difficult."

Cecelia smiled. "No apology is necessary, Your Grace."

Caroline said to Clementine, "I must say we have enjoyed having your nieces here, even though we were not always certain which was which."

"Do not feel bad. Sometimes when I have not seen them for a while, I am confused. They look as much alike as my sisters—their mothers—did. Of course, they were identical twins, not cousins. My sisters used to delight in tormenting new governesses or people they had just met by answering to one another's names. They embarrassed our mother regularly with their mistaken identity hi-jinks. It is a curious thing but the only difference between Amelia, Emmeline's mother, and Cordelia, Eleanor's mother, was the same small difference as between Eleanor and Emmeline."

"Is it something you can share with us?" Lady Beatrice leaned forward and asked.

"Auntie, are you determined to embarrass us to death?" the cousin at the duke's side asked.

"It is not something to be ashamed of, unless you want to make sure no one knows which of you is which." Clementine laughed. "Emmeline has three tiny moles in a line on her left shoulder, the same as her mother had. Eleanor has none."

Several people in the room immediately looked at the cousins who were both dressed in very modest gowns with high necklines and covered shoulders.

The cousin sitting next to Lord Simon laughed. "Looks like we can keep them guessing a little longer, sweet cousin." They exchanged knowing smiles.

Among the newly arrived guests were Cecelia and Beatrice's parents, the Earl and Countess of Glenwood.

Lady Beatrice made certain Lord William was promptly introduced to her father. The gentlemen immediately retreated to Lord Chelmsford's study for a private conversation. The lords returned shortly both smiling. Lord Glenwood stood next to his wife who was sitting in a chair near Cecelia. He bent down and whispered to her. She teared up. Lord William sat next to Beatrice, took her hand, and whispered to her. She nodded her head.

"If I could have everyone's attention," Lord Glenwood said. "I am delighted to announce William Benedict, Viscount Ashleigh, has requested my daughter, Lady Beatrice Thompson's hand in marriage. With permission of the Earl and Countess of Chelmsford, the wedding will be held here on New Year's Eve."

Lord Chelmsford smiled. "We would be delighted to host their nuptials."

"What a wonderful way to end the year," Lady Chelmsford said.

The women huddled around Beatrice hugging her while the men slapped William on the back and congratulated him. Cecelia had not moved from her chair. When the other women turned and looked at her, she moved to her sister's side, briefly hugged her, and returned to her seat with an ugly scowl on her face.

"This will be a beautiful place for a wedding," Lady Cornelia said.

"It is always good when after the business negotiations about the dowry are settled, the woman actually says yes," Lord Crestmont said.

Clementine said, "I am sure Lord Ashleigh was not surprised the lady accepted his proposal. Just look at that sweet child's face. She is marrying for love."

"Women can do that, men usually take a less emotional approach," Lord Crestmont said.

"I assure all of you. I love Beatrice and she me. I would not have cared if she came to me without anything but the clothes on her back. I intend for her dowry to be reserved for our children's needs," William said.

Beatrice blushed slightly and laid her hand on her fiancé's arm.

"Good for you," Caroline said. "The dowry is sometimes an impediment to love growing. If it becomes the focus of the marriage proposal, it takes away some of the romantic glow of the relationship."

"Most honorable men whom I know," Lord Simon began, "are not simply looking for a bankbook or a broodmare. They are looking for a lifelong partner and companion. Yes, maybe even for love. It is simply that everyone cannot afford to ignore the financial arrangements that come with a marriage."

"And let us not forget sometimes even the women themselves do not really know what, if any, dowry has been settled on them. There have been some pleasant and unpleasant surprises in the proposal process," Lord Richard said.

"Things are changing from the days of my season. My first marriage was a financial arrangement with a man who was fond of me and did no harm to me. I had to wait for my second marriage to wed for love," Clementine said with a smile.

"I am so glad it worked out for you, my sweet friend," Caroline said.

"Auntie, whom did you marry? Where is he?"

Emmeline asked.

"Me. Three days ago." Lord Crestmont stepped forward and laid his hand on his wife's shoulder. "We wanted to tell you earlier. There was not an opportunity. I hope you will be happy for us."

Both cousins moved to Clementine's side and all four of them had a family hug with tears streaming down all their faces.

Caroline hugged Clementine. "I love happy endings. I am exhausted from all this. We all need to rest a little before tonight's Christmas ball. We are having an all-evening buffet in the main dining room so people may dine at their leisure when they take a break from dancing. The orchestra begins at eight. Richard and I are looking forward to seeing all of you there."

Emmeline and Eleanor walked back to Clementine's sitting room.

"Oh, Papa, I am so happy for you both." Emmeline hugged her father. "And Auntie, this is perfect. We know you and you know us. I shall not worry about some evil woman trying to scheme away Papa's money. And best of all, Mama would be so happy you came to Papa's rescue."

"This is so wonderful. I feel like my parents have been restored to me," Eleanor said.

"I guess that means you both support our marriage?" he asked.

"Yes!" they answered in unison.

"Thank you for revealing how to tell us apart. It will help when we talk with His Grace and Lord Simon later this evening," Eleanor said.

"You told Papa our dilemma, did you not, Auntie?"

"Yes, Emmeline, I did. It made more sense to have

the whole dowry subject come up from a man."

"I am concerned about Simon's response. He has been telling me he has no need of a wife with a dowry. Do you think it is only because he knew Lady Emmeline Spenser would have one?" Eleanor asked.

"I am afraid we won't know the answer to that question until we reveal our true identities, cousin."

"If it is any comfort, Lady Caroline said Lord Summerly's situation was quite financially secure. In fact, the man most in need of a generous dowry is her own brother, the duke."

Emmeline gasped.

"Do not worry, my dear niece. She also said he was bound and determined to marry the woman he loves. He is trying to find a way for his estate to survive without a dowered wife. Caroline seemed to think he had found a solution with the Duke of Wingate, his godfather," Clementine said.

"I hate that I have caused Grey so much stress and anxiety. Why did I have such a foolish notion to test my suitors to ensure I found love? What if he is angry about my method?"

"Darling Emmeline, I am a man twice blessed. I was fortunate to marry for love both times. If this duke of yours is worthy of my daughter's love, he will understand your concerns. Maybe not immediately, but he will think about it and come to the proper conclusion."

"Oh, Papa, I hope you are correct. I could not go on living if I lost Grey's love. I cannot explain it. When he is near, I quiver with excitement. He has never kissed me, except my hand or cheek. But I cannot wait until he does." Emmeline stopped. She was red across her cheeks and down her neck. "I guess one should not talk to one's Papa about such things."

"It would probably be better for my heart if you did not. At least not until after you are properly wed." Papa hugged her tightly. Then he turned to Eleanor. "My sweet niece whom I love as if she were my own daughter, you are not a penniless orphan. Your parents made provision for you at your birth. Your mother's ample dowry was invested to be available for you when you decided to marry. Your father said it was his responsibility to care for his family."

"Oh, my. I never thought I had an inheritance."

"Papa, why not tell Eleanor sooner she had a dowry? She has been worried about being a burden to you. She was talking about taking a governess position if I married and left her."

"I am sorry I caused duress. Part of the reason was purely selfish. You and Eleanor are so like your mothers. It did my heart good, and Clementine's too, to see you together. I did not want you to be apart. I was reliving the past when Amelia and Cordelia were with us."

Eleanor hugged her uncle. "No apologies are needed. I would never have left you until Emmie decided to go. I would miss her too much. Even now, I am a little worried how we will do after we marry and are living apart from one another."

"You will be fine. You will do the same thing your mothers did," Clementine said. "You will see one another as frequently as possible. Your hearts will always carry part of the other with you."

"We may be putting the cart before the horse," Emmeline said. "First, we need to clear up who we are and then see if the gentlemen in question still want to talk to Papa."

"I am praying they do," Eleanor said.

He hugged both of them. "Do not worry. If they are wise men, they will, and I do not think either of you would have chosen a fool for a husband."

"Now, go to your rooms and get some rest. Maisie will need some time to prepare you for the ball. It is certain to be a night to remember," Clementine said.

****

The cousins stepped out of their dresses and got under the covers in their chemises. Maisie said she'd wake them in plenty of time to dress for the ball and told them to sleep so they would be well rested for the night to come.

"Ellie, are you awake?"

"Of course, I am. How can we possibly sleep when our futures are hanging on who has three tiny moles on their left shoulder?"

"I do not believe I am mistaken in my feelings for Grey or his for me."

"I am hoping Simon loves who I am and not the name I use."

"Did Shakespeare say something about smelling sweet by any name?"

"He did. I am not sure quoting him will help us, Emmie."

"Let us go and enjoy the ball and the buffet. I want to wait until later in the evening to talk to them. I would like to have the conversation in the library since that is where Grey and I really met. Will that work for you?"

"Sure, Emmie. I am all for making the reveal as romantic as possible. I know we have Auntie, your papa, and Lady Caroline on our side, but I am hoping for a little Divine intervention too. Our own huge Christmas miracle."

They must have drifted off to sleep. It seemed like only moments after praying for a miracle Maisie was shaking them awake to begin getting ready for the ball. Maisie carefully dressed Eleanor's hair into an upsweep with little curls by her cheeks and streaming down the back of her head. Then Emmeline's hairdo was made to be a carbon copy. The only difference between the cousins was Ellie had a tiara made of small diamonds and emeralds and Emmie's tiara was covered with small diamonds and rubies.

After putting on the requisite layers of crinolines, petticoats, and camisoles over their chemises and bloomers under the chemises, Maisie had Eleanor step into the center of an emerald-colored fabric pool on the floor. She pulled it to Eleanor's shoulders and began buttoning the double row of buttons down the back. The neckline was not immodest, but more festive than gowns they'd previously worn this week. An emerald lace overlay covered the snug bodice and a dramatic sweep of satin over the left shoulder cascaded to the floor behind Eleanor.

Emmeline's gown matched her cousin's except it was in vivid ruby red matching the color of the gemstones in her tiara. When both cousins had their gowns on, Maisie helped them into their dancing slippers which were dyed to match their gowns. Maisie stepped back to admire her work.

"I will have the two most beautiful Christmas gifts at the ball."

They each kissed Maisie's cheek and left for a night of dancing and revelations.

Chapter Thirteen

Eleanor and Emmeline stood at the top of the stairs and looked down at the festive decorations adorning the Great Hall. Many of the guests had arrived early and were mingling on the edge of the room away from the dancers. They waited at the top of the stairs to be announced. "Lady Emmeline Spenser and Miss Eleanor Brown." They held hands and proceeded carefully down the broad stone steps.

Lord Summerly met his lady at the base of the stairs, bowed from the waist, kissed her gloved hand, and offered his arm to escort her across the room.

Emmeline stood for a moment. Then she saw him. Greyford Parker, the Duke of Wallingford, strode across the ballroom. His black, perfectly-fitted jacket covered his broad shoulders and tapered to his narrow waist. His buff-colored breeches showed the muscular thighs beneath them running down to highly polished black boots. His vest was ruby red brocade matching the ascot tucked around his neck and under his chin. It was the same exact shade as her gown. He bowed and kissed her gloved hand. Flames of heat from his lips raced up her arm. "Miss Brown, may I have the honor of the next dance?"

"Your Grace, I would be delighted to dance with you." She made a small curtsey.

The duke swept her onto the dance floor embraced

in his strong arms as the orchestra began a waltz. She could hardly get her breath. Her stomach nervously jumped. He had such an effect on her. If only she could stay in his embrace, never having to confess the identity deception to the man she loved. She looked up to see his inky black eyes staring at her. Could he see the fear in hers? He smiled broadly. No. He had no idea what she was thinking. All she saw reflected from those dark orbs was adoration.

"I know I have said this before, but you dance divinely. I feel like we are a perfectly matched set. It is like we have been circling the floor together all of our lives."

"Thank you, Your Grace. I am simply following your lead." She felt heat flash across her cheeks.

The music stopped.

"Would you like to continue dancing or get a refreshment?"

"Dancing, please. I feel so comfortable in your arms." And as long as they were dancing she wouldn't have to tell him her foolish secret. She noticed Eleanor and Lord Summerly also stayed on the floor. Could it be for the same reason?

"I shall never object to holding you in my arms. Whether there is music or not." He winked at her.

The music began. Emmeline snuggled against his chest, closed her eyes, and breathed in his masculine scent of leather and a touch the sweet tobacco he favored. Hoping this wasn't the last night she'd get to do it. She needed to stop worrying and enjoy these moments in his arms. Fretting wouldn't change a thing.

The music stopped.

"Lady Beatrice Thompson," called the announcer.

Beatrice stood for a moment at the top of the stairs before beginning her descent. Her gown was snow white with a bright green lace bodice and border along the hem. Her hair was coiffed in an upsweep with a curl on each side of her face. She smiled radiantly and slowly glided down the steps. At the bottom of the stairs, Lord Ashleigh waited for the arrival of his fiancée. He bowed and kissed her gloved hand, then escorted her to the far side of the room.

"Lady Cecelia Thompson".

"You knew she would never share the spotlight with her sister," Emmeline whispered to her cousin.

Cecelia descended from the top of the stairs wearing a gown of iridescent deep violet. It was strapless and the amount of décolleté left no secret as to the size of her ample bosom. Matching gloves covered her hands and forearms to the elbow. She stood at the bottom of the stairs searching the hall obviously waiting to be met. Finally, her father hurried across the room and claimed her as his partner for the next dance as the band resumed playing. The scowl on her face clearly showed he was not the partner she had hoped for.

The dance ended. She took her father's arm and steered him in the Duke of Wallingford's direction. Her father bowed to 'Eleanor' and asked for the next dance with the duke's partner. His daughter stood in front of the duke. Waiting. The music began again. Grey only had eyes for his Eleanor out with Lord Glenwood.

"This is quite embarrassing. Your Grace, please, you cannot ignore me standing here," she whispered hoarsely. "We need to begin dancing or go for refreshments together."

Grey turned away from Cecelia, then back again,

and smiled.

"That is better," Cecelia said. "Shall we?" She held out her hand.

"I am sorry, Lady Cecelia, it appears someone has beat me to the punch." Grey stepped aside so Cecelia was face-to-face with her next partner.

Dark-headed Lord Edward bowed, took the still extended hand, and swept her into his arms. The expression on her face forced Grey to turn away before he began laughing aloud.

Grey insisted his partner have some punch and sit for a moment after the earl returned her to his side.

"What did you think of the news about your aunt and uncle's marriage?"

"They are a wonderful match. Both have been lost without their spouses. Aunt Clementine for five years and P…Uncle for three. I am so glad Auntie got to marry for love this time. Instead of to a dowry-hungry suitor."

"All men are not dowry hungry, even when it might be in their best interest to be so." Grey bristled. "I have taken steps to improve my financial situation. I have been hoping to discuss them with you, but we have not yet had an opportunity."

"I do not mean to cut you off, Grey, but here comes my cousin with Lord Simon. Perhaps the four of us could go into supper together. I find I am rather hungry."

"Excellent idea. We can speak more after we have eaten. I want your full attention when we talk."

Grey led the group down the hallway to the grand dining room. The buffet ran the length of the long wall from leek soup to juicy meats—venison, goose, duck, pheasant, swan—to numerous roasted vegetables to flaky fruit pies, tarts, and beautiful layered cakes dripping with sugary icing. Everyone made their selections and sat down at the far end of the table away from the other diners. They weren't isolated for long because Lady Cecelia, her sister and fiancé, and her parents came in and sat next to them.

The duke, Lord Simon, and Lord Ashleigh shared the story of their successful hunting expedition earlier Christmas morning. They had barely finished the story when Emmeline began laughing. She was watching something happening at the buffet.

At the end of the table where all the sweets were a small hand appeared from under the tablecloth. It grabbed a berry tart and disappeared back under the table. Then it came up again and took a piece of chocolate cake. Grey walked over to the buffet table. The next time the hand appeared to snatch another treat he clasped it in his own.

"Which of you is under there?" Grey demanded.

Two small boys in night clothes slowly crawled out from under the table.

"It is both of us, Uncle Grey," Oliver said sheepishly with a berry smear on his cheek. "Nanny went downstairs after she thought we were asleep."

"But we were only pretend snoring," Stephen said.

"Nanny wanted to see the dancing and all the beautiful ball gowns. She said it would be so romantic to go to a Christmas ball. We wanted to see it too 'cause we do not know what romantic means."

"So we sneaked downstairs," Stephen interrupted.

"We never saw the dancing because the food smelled so good."

"Did you not have your own Christmas supper?" Grey asked suppressing a smile.

"We did. But look at all the sweets. Miss Eleanor said they smell like heaven," Oliver said.

"But you told us they taste like heaven. Remember, Uncle Grey?" Stephen asked.

"We were not being bad," Oliver explained.

"It is Christmas and we wanted to be at the party," Stephen said with a chocolate smear on his chin.

Grey began laughing. "You are right. It is Christmas. You have had your heavenly treats. Dancing will have to wait until next year. Please go upstairs and get back in bed."

"But we do not know what romantic means yet," Oliver protested.

"That can wait a little longer too. You do not want Nanny to get in trouble, do you?"

"Oh, no, Uncle Grey." Oliver took his brother by the hand and they ran out of the room.

Grey was still laughing when he came back to the table.

"Thank you for not disciplining them," 'Eleanor' said. "It is my fault for telling them about heavenly treats."

"We have to be careful what we say in their presence. They hear and remember everything!" Grey cautioned.

"They are so adorable, especially with dirty faces."

"Hmph," Lady Cecelia said. "They are ill-mannered hooligans. Lady Chelmsford should be aghast at their behavior."

"What rot," Grey said. "Their mother and I were guilty of exactly the same thing when we were about

Oliver's age. I think it is precious to see family history repeating itself. Lady Chelmsford would have laughed right along with me. How can my nephews be badly behaved when they make me smile? Did you never do anything wrong as a child, Lady Cecelia?"

"No. I have always behaved impeccably," Cecelia insisted.

"Except in grottos and when playing Whist or charades," 'Emmeline' said under her breath.

'Eleanor' had to stifle a laugh when she realized Grey and Simon both heard her cousin's true comment.

"Are you ready for more dancing?" Simon asked.

"We would like you to come with us first," 'Eleanor' said extending her hand to Grey.

"Where are we going?" Grey asked.

"To finish our conversation."

"All four of us?" the duke asked raising an eyebrow.

"Yes, it will all make sense soon."

'Eleanor' walked past Cecelia's chair. Suddenly, the woman pushed her chair away from the table and stood up in front of Grey. Then she awkwardly lurched into his arms.

"Oh, Your Grace, you saved me from falling and embarrassing myself. Thank you," Cecelia gushed.

Grey did not respond. He grasped Cecelia by her forearms and moved her out of his path.

"But, Your Grace, do you not want to make certain I am unharmed?"

Grey said nothing and took 'Eleanor's' hand.

"She never gives up," Grey whispered to his love.

'Eleanor' led the way into the library. 'Emmeline' closed the door after them. The gentlemen looked confused.

"Please have a seat. We have something important to tell you," 'Eleanor' began. Grey and Simon sat down. The cousins stood in front of them.

"There has been a great deal of discussion these last couple of days about dowries," 'Emmeline' said.

"Yes," Simon jumped out of his chair. "And I have made it abundantly clear they are not important to me."

"I was trying to explain to you earlier, Eleanor, I have made arrangements to ensure you have a stable financial future with me, should you accept my offer of marriage…when I officially make it," Grey said.

"We understand where you both stand on dowries or lack thereof," 'Emmeline' said. "Please sit back down, Simon."

"We hope you understand how important it is to my cousin and to me that we marry for love regardless of our personal money situation," 'Eleanor' said. "It may seem silly to you, but I especially wanted to know finances would not play a part in my selection of a future husband. Not my money or his. So we devised a plan to ensure love would triumph."

"I am totally confused," Grey said. "Eleanor, why would you think someone would marry you for your money? Are you not without a dowry?"

The cousins looked at one another and nodded in unison.

"Do you recall what our Aunt Clementine revealed about how to tell us apart?"

"I do not need to look at your left shoulder. I am not confused. I know which one of you I love," Grey said angrily. "Your aunt is wrong. There are lots of other differences between you, subtle differences. The way your eyes twinkle when you are doing something mischievous with my nephews. Eleanor, you have an extra titter when you laugh. Just one syllable longer than your cousin's. I have never been uncertain about which one of you I love."

"Wallingford is right. You are not exactly the same. I would never mistake Emmeline for Eleanor. I fail to understand what you are telling us. I would love you, Emmeline, if you had not a pence to your name."

"Would you love us by other names?"

"Of course, I love the woman, not the name," Grey said. "Where is all this going?"

"Simon, please come closer," Eleanor said. Simon got up again and walked to her side. When he was next to her with his back to Grey, she carefully pulled down the left shoulder of her gown. Simon's eyes widened. He brushed his hand across her shoulder and smiled broadly.

Before he could speak, Emmeline took Grey's hand and pulled him to his feet closer to her. She tugged on the left shoulder of her gown until three tiny moles appeared in a row. Grey stared into her tear-filled eyes, reached up to her shoulder, and gently rubbed his thumb over the three dark dots.

"I never meant to cause you concern worrying about how to provide for me. I witnessed the difference between my parents' marriage for love and my aunt's first financially-arranged marriage. My parents were blissfully happy. I want that kind of relationship. I want forever happiness. With you. Please say something, Grey." His hand rested on her shoulder. His face was unreadable.

"I shall say something," Simon spoke. "It makes no

difference to me. Not a bit. Eleanor Brown, I love you and I want to marry you. I may not have known the right name, but I definitely have the right woman for me."

Eleanor hugged him. "I am glad to hear you say so. The surprise is I do have a dowry—apparently a substantial one—my uncle has been managing it until I marry."

"Let us go find your uncle and speak with him now."

"Tomorrow is soon enough," Eleanor protested.

Simon nodded at Emmeline and Grey who had stood frozen in place since the revelation. Eleanor nodded and they left the room.

Tears overflowed running down Emmeline's cheeks. Grey reached up and swept them away with his thumb. He stared into her green eyes and smiled.

"Please, no crying. I am trying to reconcile all this. I understand why you began the ruse, it is a reasonable thing for an heiress to do. But once you knew that I only had eyes for you despite Cecelia Thompson's shenanigans, why did you not confide in me? Tell me the truth? Why let it go so long?"

"Grey, it has not been so long. We only met five days ago and it was just four days ago when you rescued me in this very room. Eleanor was not certain what Simon's situation was and she feared he would give her up when he discovered she was not an heiress. She did not know about her inheritance until this afternoon after Papa and Aunt Clementine arrived."

"You are right. It only seems as if I have known you forever. This marriage house party was Caroline's idea. I came strictly to appease her."

"If you remember, I was looking at books because I wanted no part in the husband-hunting party. I told you so in this very room."

Grey chuckled. "Yes, you did. Were you uncertain about my feelings for you? My intentions?"

"Frankly, yes. Until we came out of the fortune teller's tent. Then you stunned me. I could hardly believe you referred to me as the mother of your children. I wanted to believe it was true love. I knew it was from my side. Why not simply ask me to marry you instead of alluding to me being your dancing duchess and such?"

"Do not laugh. When the gypsy said there must be no secrets between us, I thought she was talking directly to me. I thought it meant I needed to get my finances straightened out before I could face your guardian to ask for your hand in marriage. I went and talked with the Duke of Wingate almost immediately. He is my godfather and was my father's best friend. He had the solution. My mother had given her best jewelry to him to hold for Thomas' wife. She was afraid if he inherited it directly, he would give it to one of his many mistresses and it would no longer be in the family. My godfather still had it. It has considerable value and would certainly come in handy if I married the dowry-less Miss Brown."

"I am feeling a little better to learn you were keeping a secret too. How do you feel about talking to Lady Emmeline Spenser's father about her hand instead of Eleanor's?"

"I intend to do it first thing in the morning."

"Why not now?"

"Because first I am going to do something I have

wanted to do since you fell off the library ladder and into my arms."

Grey put his hand under her chin, tipped her head back, and put an arm around her waist. Her green eyes sparkled. He pulled her closer. Her soft breath brushed against his cheeks. He inhaled her rose scent. Then gently, sweetly, he kissed her on those luscious pink lips. When he released her, Emmeline pulled him back to her, stood on tiptoe, and tipped his head toward her until she connected with his lips. She kissed him. Longer and harder than his kiss had been.

"I knew there were benefits to loving a saucy wench!"

Emmeline's cheeks burned bright red. She stayed snuggled in his embrace.

"You are so easy to tease, my dear. Oh, we have not talked about when you want to marry. Are you in favor of long engagements or short ones?"

"I think we should marry on New Year's Eve. Beatrice and William's wedding is scheduled for then. While the vicar is here, we could marry too. I expect my cousin and Lord Simon will do the same. I cannot wait too long to become a married woman."

"What is the rush about marrying?"

"I am anxious to see what happens after the kissing part."

"I have created a monster. You are incorrigible, my love. We had best get back to the ballroom before your eagerness sweeps me into doing something untoward."

He offered his arm to her.

The rest of the night was pure bliss. Grey and Emmeline stayed wrapped in each other's arms, as did Simon and Eleanor. The gentlemen agreed they would speak with Lord Spenser together in the morning after breakfast.

****

"Ellie, when are you and Simon planning to marry?"

"New Year's Eve when William and Beatrice do."

"Perfect. Us too. It looks like we got our Christmas miracle. Papa is sure to approve our matches tomorrow. Our mamas are so happy looking down at us. Merry Christmas, Ellie."

"Merry Christmas, Emmie."

Chapter Fourteen

Simon and Grey had their heads together as they sat at one end of the table when the cousins walked into the breakfast room.

"Good morning, ladies. I trust you slept well." Simon jumped up to pull out a chair for Eleanor and Grey did the same for Emmeline. The ladies were seated across the table from their intendeds.

"I was too excited to fall asleep immediately," Eleanor confessed.

"I am glad. So was I." Simon reached for her hand across the table.

"And how did my lady Emmeline sleep last night?"

"Quite well, Your Grace. And you?"

"Like a rock. My decision has been made. I have nothing to torment me now when I close my eyes."

Emmeline smiled. "Truth is a powerful sleep aid."

"Amen," Grey agreed.

More guests wandered into the room. Their discussion turned to the weather and tired feet from dancing the last two nights out of three. Lord and Lady Crestmont joined them at the table.

"Good morning, Papa, Auntie."

"Good morning, my dears," Clementine said.

"I had not expected people to be up and around so early this morning after such a long night of dancing," Lord Crestmont said.

"We have a lot to do today," Eleanor said with a blush.

"Let us not get the cart before the horse, cousin dear. We hope we have a lot to do," Emmeline corrected her.

"Lord Crestmont, after you have finished your breakfast, the duke and I would like to see you for a private discussion on matters of the utmost importance," Lord Simon said.

Lord Crestmont raised an eyebrow. "You both want to see me? I wonder what it could be regarding." He winked.

"Uncle, you are a scallywag."

"Papa, hurry and finish your tea. I think you are deliberately dragging this out."

"You are in a rush for me to meet with a young man? What happened to the little girl who was never going to marry? Who had no interest in husband hunting and was never going to leave her poor papa all alone?"

"You have Auntie now, so you are no longer by yourself. Things have changed. Do you not want Ellie and me to be happy too?"

"My darling daughter, your happiness is the thing I most desire. Gentlemen, perhaps we may borrow Chelmsford's study for our conversation."

"I am sure my brother-in-law would be happy to facilitate our discussion. If you will excuse me, I shall find him and confirm its availability." Grey stood and bowed slightly then went to find Richard.

By the time Lord Crestmont finished breakfast, the duke had returned. The three gentlemen excused themselves and retired to the study.

"I could not be happier," Clementine gushed. "Your mamas would be so delighted to see the two of you married on the same day, just as they were. Are you planning for New Year's Eve since the vicar will be here for Lady Beatrice and Lord William's nuptials?"

"Assuming Papa says yes and the gentlemen officially ask us today, yes."

"We see no reason for a long engagement," Ellie said.

"I hoped coming to Lady Chelmsford's holiday house party would introduce you to new suitors. I had no idea that things would fall into place so quickly," Clementine said.

"Let us not be totally delighted until Simon and Grey come out of the study and actually propose to us," Emmie said.

"You worry too much, cousin dear. When things are meant to be, they will happen. Our weddings are fated. Auntie, would you walk with me into the Great Hall to talk about decorations? Then we need to talk with Lady Beatrice to coordinate for the joint ceremony," Eleanor said.

"I would be happy to. Are you coming, Emmeline?"

"No, Auntie, you two go ahead. I am going to hover outside the study to get the news as soon as it is available. I hope it is good."

Emmeline left the breakfast room and paced in the hallway a short distance from Lord Richard's study.

"What are you doing lurking around here?" Lady Cecelia asked shrilly when she met Emmeline in the hall.

"I do not believe it is any of your business."

"Oh, how pathetic. The poor little orphan girl thinks she is about to rope a duke into marriage." Cecelia cackled. "No matter what your guardian says, this is not over. The Duke of Wallingford still has time to see the light and you will be left holding a bouquet with no groom at your side. I intend to make certain of it. Instead he will be at my side. I will be the next Duchess of Wallingford." Cecelia walked past Emmeline with a snort.

She still thinks I'm Eleanor. Her information is woefully out of date. Grey made it clear to me Cecelia would be the last person he would consider marrying. How can she be so confident he isn't marrying me but her?

The door to the study opened. Emmeline stepped back into a doorway. She didn't want Grey to know she was worried about the outcome of their discussion. Simon and Grey stepped into the hall.

"Thank you, gentlemen," Lord Crestmont said.

They shook hands all around. Simon and Grey walked in the direction away from Emmeline's hiding place. She stepped out of the doorway and ran into the study.

"Oh, Papa. What is the news?"

"I believe it is exactly what you wanted to hear. Lord Summerly has requested Eleanor's hand in marriage."

"What else?"

"I approved his request. I believe they are well-suited and will be quite happy."

"Papa, what else?"

"What am I forgetting?"

"What about the duke? Did he ask you anything?"

"Oh, yes he did. He asked to have my most precious daughter's hand so she could become his duchess." Papa smiled and pulled his daughter into an embrace. "You are going to say yes are you not?"

"Yes, Papa. I am. I never knew I could feel about anyone the way I feel about Grey. Was this how Mama felt about you?"

"I would like to think it was. The duke is quite in love with you as well. He made sure I knew he had made financial arrangements beyond your dowry. My little girl is becoming a duchess. Amelia would be so proud. Clementine will be too. Lady Chelmsford is one of her dearest friends. Speaking of Clementine, where is she? And Eleanor?"

"They are off wedding planning, I think."

"Should we join them?"

"Papa, I need to find Grey. I want to make sure I get an official proposal first."

"My little worry wart. Go! Your precious duke probably is not too far away. I will find my wife and niece."

Emmeline raced down the hall in the direction Grey had gone. She spotted him in an alcove at the end of the hall. He was standing almost toe-to-toe with someone—a woman. Then she heard the cackle. She saw Cecelia's face peek over Grey's shoulder. She couldn't hear what Grey was saying. She moved closer. She listened.

Cecelia threw her arms around Grey's neck. "Oh darling, I can be ready in less than an hour. We can be to Gretna Green before that little doxy knows you have come to your senses. I warned her you did not love her." Cecelia raised her voice. And watched Emmeline as she spoke.

Emmeline gasped loudly enough that Grey turned around as he pulled Cecelia's arms off his neck.

"Darling, I was coming to find you before I was rudely intercepted," Grey said.

"You were? To tell me you are running away with this harpy after you just asked Papa for my hand? How could you betray me like this?" Tears rolled down Emmeline's cheeks. "I thought you loved me."

Cecelia cackled and tried to loop her arm through Grey's. He stepped away from her. "Emmeline, this is not what it looks like. I promise. Cecelia wants you to believe a lie. I do not love her, I never even considered her for marriage. I love you. Only you. Please." He reached toward her.

Emmeline turned and ran away from Grey's outstretched arms.

Grey faced Cecelia. "Are you totally insane? How many ways do I need to say I am not marrying you? Not ever. If you have hurt Emmeline with your nonsense I cannot think how to punish you and still be considered a gentleman."

"Oh, you love me, dear duke. You just do not know it yet. Come New Year's Eve, I will be the one saying 'I Do' at your side. Not Miss Brown. Wait, you are calling her Emmeline. She is the earl's daughter, not the orphan cousin? No matter. I have a dowry that is triple hers. Think about all the things we could do with my money."

"Lady Cecelia, and I use the term loosely, it would not matter to me if your dowry was one hundred times what hers is. I do not and never will love you. Get it through your head. If Emmeline refuses to have me now, I will not marry at all on New Year's Eve. I will never marry until she agrees to be mine. Leave me alone. I have to find her."

Grey followed after Emmeline hoping to catch her and explain Cecelia's absurd charade.

"My dear duke, I am not finished yet. You have no idea who you are dealing with. I intend to be the Duchess of Wallingford to begin the new year." Cecelia cackled to herself as she sashayed down the hall.

Grey had to find Emmeline. He couldn't imagine what she must think after seeing Cecelia draped over him cackling and spouting nonsense about running away to Gretna Green. He thought when he told Cecelia he'd asked for Emmeline's hand she would back off, instead she seemed more determined than ever to embarrass him into marrying her. The woman was completely unhinged. No amount of mortification would force him into a lifetime with that witch.

Emmeline was not in her room. Maisie answered the door and said she hadn't seen the lady since before breakfast although she had been away from the room for her own meal in the servant's quarters. Lord Crestmont's suite was empty except for the earl's valet. Grey found Eleanor and Simon with Emmeline's father and aunt in the Great Hall discussing wedding decorations with Caroline, Beatrice, and William. Caroline walked over to him.

"Here he is. Where is Emmeline? Did you pop the question? Did she say yes? We wondered if you two wanted to have input on the decorating plans for the triple wedding." Caroline kissed her brother's cheek. "Congratulations."

"The celebration of my marriage is premature. I seem to have misplaced my bride-to-be."

"What do you mean? Where is my cousin? Did you not propose to her?" Eleanor asked.

"Thanks to Lady Cecelia's shenanigans, I never had the opportunity. She drove Emmeline away and I am afraid my darling may have thought Cecelia's spoutings about us eloping were the truth." Grey explained the debacle in the hallway.

Beatrice came to him and laid her hand on his forearm. "I apologize, Your Grace. I am afraid my older sister has become slightly deranged. She is determined to marry you and only you. She believes she can will it to happen, regardless of any plans you have to the contrary. Until you are legally wed to someone else, I am not sure any force on earth can deter her from those misguided notions. Surely, Lady Emmeline did not believe what Cecelia said."

Eleanor sniffled. "I am afraid Emmeline might have believed her. She keeps saying she can hardly believe she has actually found a man who loves her as much as she loves him. She seems to be holding her breath waiting for the whole thing to explode. She thought it would happen when His Grace learned we had switched identities. When it did not and the duke wanted to meet with her father, I think she imagined all kinds of other reasons why he would no longer love her. I know it is not any more rational than Cecelia's ideas, but who thinks straight when they are in love?"

Simon came to Eleanor's side and held her hand. "Do not worry. Your cousin will soon realize she will be getting married at the same time as you are."

"She needs some time and space. I think we should

wait to search for her. She has to be somewhere in the castle. The weather is too forbidding for her to leave. Let us wait until luncheon. If she does not appear then we can start looking for her in earnest. Hopefully, given the chance, she will realize she is creating bogeymen and Your Grace has every intention of marrying her," Clementine recommended.

"I have to find her. She cannot possibly believe any of the lies Cecelia spewed. Does she not have faith in me? How can I convince her how much I love her? Please help me find Emmeline," Grey pleaded.

"Your Grace, I am afraid my sweet wife is correct. My daughter can be incredibly stubborn when she feels she has been wronged. And if she is also embarrassed at being thrown over for Lady Cecelia, it will be even worse. She has probably found an isolated corner somewhere on the grounds and is licking her wounds. She will not be rushed. It is a waste of breath to argue with her when she is in this state." Lord Crestmont patted Grey on the back.

"Yes, yes. I will wait. I am not happy with the delay, but you know your daughter better than I do. I shall see you at the luncheon."

Grey excused himself and left the Great Hall. The others stayed and continued their planning for the upcoming weddings. Caroline and Eleanor decided that between them they could come up with decorations Grey and Emmeline would approve of.

Chapter Fifteen

Emmeline ran down the hall, down the stairs, and out of the keep. The cold wind slapped her wet cheeks when she ran onto the bailey. How could she have been so wrong about Grey? She needed to be alone. To calm down. To stop crying. Where could she go? She was almost to the stables and quickened her pace to reach them. It was much too dismal a day for anyone to go riding. Maybe she could be alone there.

The stablemaster was on the other end of the aisle in front of the stalls. He was in an animated conversation with one of the grooms. He never saw her. She ducked into the first stall she came to. Winter Beauty, the snow-white filly was standing at her mother's side vigorously nursing. The mare nickered at Emmeline. She petted the animal's back and walked to her head. The horse nuzzled her shoulder. Emmeline stroked its velvety nose.

"What a beautiful baby you have. She is growing so fast." The mare nudged her toward the filly who had stopped nursing and stood staring at Emmeline. "Yes. You are well-named, Winter Beauty." She stooped down and hugged the filly around the neck. Tears started flowing again. Grey named this little one.

It had been then that she fell instantly in love with him. He was so loving, so comfortable with his nephews. The filly wiggled out of her embrace leaving

Emmeline squatting on the ground. The mare whinnied loudly. A stable boy opened the stall door.

"Forgive me, my lady. I did not know anyone was in here. It is not a fit day to be riding. You were not going out, were you?" he asked.

Embarrassed, Emmeline brushed the tears off her cheeks with the back of her hand and stood. "No, I did not want to ride. Just wanted to see the new arrival. I shall leave now."

It was getting colder. Where could she hide? A place no one would find her? The tower room. She raced across the bailey and up the narrow twisting stairs. She had to stop part way to the top to get her breath. Sobbing is not conducive to easy breathing. Neither is running on the stairs. Her tears would not stop.

Once she was breathing more easily, she continued to the top. Someone had been there since yesterday morning. Perry and the boys had carefully closed the door and secured it. Now the bar was off to the side. The heavy oak door was partially ajar. Who would leave it open? She was able to wedge herself into the crack and push the barrier out enough to gain access to the room.

A brisk north wind blew through the windows. She looked out across the Pennine foothills to Scotland. Would Grey and Cecelia be on their way to Gretna Green soon? Why ask Papa for her hand if that was his plan all along? It was so embarrassing. She'd made such a fool of herself over finding "The One", of being totally in love with him. It didn't make sense. Grey had never shown himself to be conniving and cruel, unlike Lady Cecelia Thompson. She was a witch in every sense of the word.

It was so cold. Too breezy to stand by the window. She slipped to the floor behind a chair in the warmest nook in the tower. Her tear-soaked handkerchief did little to capture the tears continuing to fall. She couldn't think straight. Every time she closed her eyes she saw Cecelia wrapped in Grey's arms—the place Emmeline was supposed to be and only Emmeline. For the rest of her life.

Cecelia had to be lying about eloping. About Grey wanting her as his duchess. About everything. It wouldn't be the first time. She had been on a mission to thwart Grey's interest in Emmeline or anyone else, from the beginning. Emmeline wanted to believe Cecelia was the villain. Her love of Grey would win out in the end. Wouldn't it?

Had Emmeline only known the charming Duke of Wallingford, Greyford Parker, for less than a week? How much could she understand about his true nature in such a short amount of time? If Grey had wanted a way out of marrying her, if he wanted to be free to marry Cecelia, why didn't he announce it when he learned she had deceived him? She was not Miss Eleanor Brown. He would have had a good excuse to discontinue their relationship. It was the perfect out. There was more here than she could fathom. She was tired. Emotionally spent. What would she do? What could she? She didn't want to embarrass Aunt Clementine or her father and she certainly didn't want Eleanor to give up her Lord Summerly because of Emmeline's tragic circumstances.

Suddenly she heard a loud grunt and the massive door slammed shut with a boom. Before Emmeline could get off the floor she heard the bar fall into place blocking the door closed. Someone had intentionally trapped her in the tower room. With the bar in place she had no way to escape. The door wouldn't budge at all.

She screamed and beat on the massive barrier. Her cries echoed around the room but no one could hear her since she was so far above the ground. She went to the window and cried out. The only person in the bailey was Lady Cecelia—running as fast as she could away from the bottom of the tower. She was the one who had slammed the door. If Grey was planning to go to Gretna Green with Cecelia, why would she need to lock Emmeline away where no one would find her? How could she be so cold-blooded? So eager to harm Emmeline? She must have been worried the duke wouldn't leave with her unless Emmeline couldn't be found.

****

Grey was the first person at the table for luncheon. He kept a steady watch on the doorway. Hoping each time he heard feminine footfalls coming down the hall they would belong to Emmeline. Every sound was a false alarm. None of the steps were hers.

Lady Chelmsford came in the room and sat down next to him. "I hate to see my brother looking so forlorn."

"I hope it is a temporary state. I promise I will not stop smiling as soon as Emmeline walks in the room."

"I believe you got the true love you asked for."

"Indeed, Caro, I did. I am beginning to wonder if it would be easier on one's heart to marry for money than for love."

"I can answer that," Lady Clementine said. "It may

seem easier on the surface, but you miss out on so much. Better to have a few scars on your heart than to never know the richness of feeling that causes them." She patted Grey's back as she passed him. "Do not abandon all hope yet."

****

Lunch was over and no Emmeline. They agreed to start searching for her in an organized way. Grey went to the stables first. He was assured no one had taken a horse out. It was too cold and slick under foot for the stablemaster to allow anyone, no matter how experienced a rider, to travel outside the castle grounds today.

Grey turned to leave when one of the stable boys called to him.

"Your Grace, there was a lady here visiting the new filly earlier this morning. Is she the one you are looking for?"

"Possibly, can you describe her?"

"She was about my height, chestnut hair, and the greenest eyes I have ever seen, begging pardon for noticing, Your Grace." The young man's face reddened.

"No pardon necessary. She is who I am seeking. If she comes back, send someone for me immediately and do not let her leave, please."

****

Emmeline had fallen asleep. Exhausted, cold, and aching she slowly stood. She heard noise rising from the bailey below. People were calling her name. She looked out the window. Grey strode out of the stables. Cecelia ran to meet him. She hugged him tightly and kissed his cheek. They must be preparing to leave. Grey looked angry. Why would he be unhappy when he was getting the woman he wanted? She did not need to see more. She slid back to the floor. More tears. No one would know she was trapped in the freezing cold tower until it was too late. It was getting colder by the minute.

Grey pulled away from Cecelia's unwanted embrace without a word to her. She turned and ran back into the keep. Emmeline didn't see his reaction to Cecelia's affection.

There was a noise at the door. Someone was coming to rescue her. The bar clattered to the floor. The door groaned loudly as it slowly opened only a crack. Then it stopped moving. Steps raced down the stairs. Emmeline glimpsed a man's back. A green jacket. Black hair.

"Please, open the door the rest of the way," she called after the disappearing figure. He didn't return. She looked down to the bailey. Who had helped her? She saw a figure quickly moving toward the stables. Who was it? She didn't recognize him from behind. She couldn't see his face. Only Grey and Lord Edward had black hair. She would have known Grey, even from the back. Why would Edward want to help her? To undo the harm Cecelia tried to do her?

****

The duke was halfway back to the keep from the stable when Oliver and Stephen met him. "Uncle Grey, would you like us to check the tower room for Miss Brown?" Oliver asked.

"You mean, Lady Emmeline, remember?" Stephen said.

"Uncle Grey knows who I mean."

"A great idea. I will go with you. You might need help with the door."

The boys ran across the bailey to the base of the tower. Lady Cecelia came out of the keep and intercepted the duke before he could follow them. She threw her arms around his neck again. He argued a few moments and she moved closer. Finally, he jerked her arms down and shoved her away from him. She stood in front of him howling loudly. Then she slapped his face and fled back inside. Grey hurried to join his nephews at the tower entrance.

****

Emmeline charged at the door throwing all her weight against it. Creak. A fraction farther ajar. After three more attempts it had opened enough for her to slip out. Her gown caught on something. She was stuck. She couldn't return into the tower room or get completely out the door. She heard voices on the stairs. She had to get free. She didn't want to be imprisoned again. She jerked her dress. She tore it. She had no choice. At least she was free. Maisie could repair whatever the damage was when she got back to her room. If she went back. Where could she hide?

****

"Hurry, Uncle Grey, the door is too heavy for me to open by myself," Oliver announced.

The boys burst into the tower room as soon as Grey swung the door fully open. No one was in the room.

"Uncle, I think this belongs to a lady," Stephen said picking up a lacy handkerchief. "It is wet and cold."

"Yes, it belongs to Emmeline. She has been here. Not too long ago. We should check her room again," Grey quickly led the boys back down the steps.

When silence filled the room, Emmeline slowly

stepped out from behind the oversized chest in the hall. She brushed the cobwebs and dust from her hair. She shook her skirts to remove the dirt.

Why hadn't she revealed herself? It was Grey with Oliver and Stephen. Why hadn't he left with Cecelia yet? Did he care where Emmeline was? Had Cecelia confessed to locking her in the tower room? They didn't seem to know she had been there until they found her handkerchief. No, Cecelia would never confess, not if she thought Grey was close to eloping with her. It was too cold to stay in the tower hallway much longer. She would have pneumonia for certain. But where to go?

****

The hothouse erased all traces of the chill of the tower. Now she was too warm. She'd be ill for certain with all these rapid temperature changes.

Hobbs was trimming bushes when he surprised Emmeline huddled in the corner of the hothouse near the Lady Caroline Winter rose.

"My lady, are you hurt?" The gardener knelt next to her.

"No, Hobbs. I am sorry, I did not mean to frighten you."

"Do you know His Grace and the others are looking for you? They were here earlier."

"I guess this is not a good place for me to stay. I will be going."

Hobbs stood up. "Stay right where you are, my lady. I will go get His Grace. Please do not move. They are all very worried about you."

Hobbs dropped his pruners and ran out of the hothouse.

She couldn't face Grey. Not until she knew the truth about Cecelia and her duke. But where could she hide now?

The cold air took her breath away when she stepped out of the hothouse. If she was planning to go anywhere outside of the keep she would need warmer clothes. She stepped into the shadows when she saw Grey follow Hobbs into the hothouse. She only needed a few minutes to retrieve her cape and bonnet.

It sounded like everyone was in the gold salon. She crept up the stairs and into her room. She had the warm clothes in hand and opened the door when someone gasped behind her. Maisie.

"Lady Emmeline, please do not go."

"I must. Please do not give me away. Please promise me."

Maisie nodded. Emmeline slipped out the door.

Chapter Sixteen

There were a lot of long faces at tea. Caroline tried to be upbeat and hopeful but the castle had been scoured from top to bottom. Emmeline had been sighted in the stables and the hothouse. Her handkerchief was found in the tower, but they were always a step behind her. No Emmeline yet.

"Perhaps she struck out on foot to a nearby cottage," Cecelia said rather too cheerfully for the rest of the guests. "Maybe she ran away because she does not want to marry you, Your Grace. It is a lady's prerogative to change her mind. Even she can see how much you love me."

"Cecelia, please keep your opinions to yourself," Beatrice scolded her sister.

"Emmeline would not leave without telling me goodbye. I assure you, she is still here. Somewhere. And you will not convince me she has changed her mind about marrying the duke," Eleanor protested.

"If she did leave, she would not have gone without getting her cape and bonnet. It would be suicide to go outside without a wrap in this weather," Clementine said.

"Fetch Maisie. She will know if Emmeline left the keep," Lord Crestmont ordered.

A few minutes later, a tearful Maisie came into the gold salon. She curtsied to Lord and Lady Crestmont.

"What did you need, my lord?" she asked without looking at her master.

"Did Lady Emmeline come back to her room at any point this afternoon?" Lord Crestmont asked.

The maid hesitated.

"Please, Maisie. She may be in danger," Eleanor said.

"Oh, it is my fault. I asked her to stay but she refused. I could not tell anyone because she made me promise not to give her away. I am so sorry."

Clementine patted the young woman's back. "Thank you for telling us the truth now. You may return to the room."

"If she got her cape and bonnet, she is no longer in the castle. I should go and check the village. She could be hurt or lost on the path," Grey said as he rose from his chair.

"Paul and I will go with you. You do not know the area as well as we do. We should take the sleigh in case Lady Emmeline needs help returning to the castle," Richard said.

"It is getting so late. Is it prudent to go out in the dark?" Caroline asked.

"The better question is whether it is safe to leave Emmeline in the dark if she did venture out on the trail," Grey insisted.

"I was jesting," Lady Cecelia said. "Even Lady Emmeline is not foolish enough to risk her life to escape. Taking her wrap was part of her ruse. She would stay here in the warm. I am sure she is somewhere nearby laughing at us and all the havoc she is creating."

"I am certain she is not here," Grey growled. "Nor

is she laughing."

****

Grey drove the sleigh. Richard led the way on horseback and Paul rode behind Grey. There were small footprints tracking across the field on the other side of the drawbridge. It was impossible to determine how long ago they were made. Richard followed them in the bright light of the full moon.

Grey spotted something sticking up from the snow along the trail. It was black. He stopped the sleigh. The snow was trampled down as if someone or something had fallen there. He carefully pulled the item out of the glistening white powder. A woman's glove. He couldn't remember what color Emmeline's gloves were. Why hadn't he paid attention? It had to be hers. This must be the right track.

They continued down the path carefully watching for clues on both sides of the road. They reached the first cottage on the edge of the village. Flickering, yellow candlelight showed through the windows and black smoke billowed above the chimney. Richard thought it would be less overwhelming if he approached the home alone. The villagers knew him. Paul less so and Grey hardly at all.

Lord Chelmsford rapped loudly on the heavy wooden door. It slowly opened.

"My lord, I wondered if it might be you coming out at this hour and in the cold. Please come in."

The door opened wide. Lord Chelmsford shook the man's hand and followed him into the warm cottage. "Good to see you, John Harper. If you were expecting me, I am guessing you must have seen the young woman we are searching for."

"Aye, that we did." The villager took a long draw on his pipe.

"How long ago did she stop here?"

" 'Twas over three hours ago, sire."

"Which way did she go when she left your house?"

"She did not leave us yet. She be fast asleep in the far corner over yon."

The earl saw a form covered in blankets on a pallet on the floor in the corner farthest from the door.

Mrs. Harper sat in a chair by the fire. She put down her knitting. "The poor little lamb was frightened to death, cold, wet, and hungry. I got her out of those clothes and into one of my gowns. It was far too big for such a small slip of a thing, but her dress needed to dry. I wrapped her in one of my shawls and fed her three bowlfuls of good bone broth."

"Thank you for your kindness. I am happy to pay for whatever she ate."

"Not necessary, my lord," Harper said. "We would do the same for anyone who came by in such a state as her."

"Mrs. Harper, you said she was frightened. Did she say what of or why?"

"From what I could piece together between her sobs, she was running away because the man she loves and wants to marry has eloped to Gretna Green with another. She is embarrassed and heartsick. She could not stay and face everyone else once the news was well-known around the castle," Mrs. Harper explained.

"Unfortunately, she had reasons to believe that story. Let me assure you, nothing could be further from the truth. The man she loves is outside. There is no other woman. The duke came to find her and to ask her to marry him."

" 'Tis a blessing. Will be good to see her smile again. She was such a merry soul at the Christmas feast at Winterhaven. I recognized her right away when I opened the door even though she was pale as the snow," Mrs. Harper said.

"We brought the sleigh with us to take her back to Winterhaven."

"My lord, would you let the lamb rest until morning? She has cried until she had no tears left. I am believin' she would not want His Grace to see her like she looks right now. Perhaps her gentleman could come for her tomorrow morning after she is well-rested and fresher," Mrs. Harper suggested.

"We can keep her busy here until he comes to fetch her," Mr. Harper assured the earl.

"An excellent idea. I will ask the duke to return in the morning. Many thanks for taking care of my brother-in-law's future bride. I am certain Lady Chelmsford will want to personally thank you. Good night."

Richard went outside to bring Paul and Grey up to date on Emmeline's adventure.

"I cannot leave her here all alone," Grey said. "I will wait with the sleigh and see her at first light."

"Do not be foolish. She is not alone. The Harpers have made her quite comfortable and she is sound asleep. You will freeze staying all night out here. The Harpers do not have any extra beds. You need your supper and a good night's rest. Your declarations of undying love will keep until tomorrow morning. Your sister would have my head if I left you here. Come on. We will be home in time for dinner."

The duke went to Lord Crestmont's suite immediately after returning to Winterhaven. Lord Randolph, Lady Clementine, Eleanor, and Simon were together in the sitting room. Grey told them the good news that Emmeline had been found—cold and hungry but basically unharmed from her adventure. He shared his plans for after he retrieved his bride-to-be tomorrow morning. Everyone was relieved Emmeline had not been hurt.

"Cecelia Thompson should be thrashed within an inch of her life," Eleanor said angrily. "She has been taunting Emmeline all week, especially since she thought she was me—an untitled nobody. She announced the first day we met that she would be leaving Winterhaven as a duchess. Your duchess, Your Grace."

"Please call me Grey. You are almost Emmeline's sister which means you will be the closest thing I shall have to a sister-in-law. You are right about Cecelia. She has been the creator of a lot of the confusion here. I cannot be too angry with her though. Her joke about Emmeline leaving the castle turned out to be what happened. I believe Cecelia will regret saying that when she learns it is indeed where Emmeline was and that I am more determined to marry her than ever. Cecelia Thompson was never going to be my duchess anywhere except in her deranged mind."

****

Only Lady Cecelia frowned when Lord Chelmsford shared the news Lady Emmeline had been found in the village unharmed. The duke thanked her profusely for the idea of checking outside the castle for the missing woman.

"Did she remain in the village because she does not wish to marry you, Your Grace?" Cecelia asked.

"I do not know what the lady's desires are. I was not able to speak with her this evening. I plan to see her first thing tomorrow morning so we can plan our next steps. Together," Grey said.

"I see." Lady Cecelia licked her bottom lip, then smiled broadly. "Best of luck, Your Grace."

It had been an emotionally exhausting day for everyone. Most guests retired to their rooms shortly after dessert. Grey went to the Duke of Wingate's room. He wanted to discuss his plan with his godfather. Wingate welcomed him and poured them both a brandy to enjoy while they talked in front of the fire. The conversation stretched into several hours.

"Thank you. I wanted to discuss my plan with an impartial third party. I appreciate your insights and your blessing," Grey said.

"Thank you for asking me. I could not be prouder of you if you had been my own son. She is a beautiful woman who obviously loves you. Any woman who would want you to have your heart's desire ahead of her own is a love to hold for the rest of your life."

"I intend to do exactly that. Thank you. For the fatherly advice and the timely inheritance. Especially Mother's ring."

****

It was after midnight. Lady Cecelia crept down the hallway clad only in a thin dressing robe. Her long blonde hair fell loosely across her shoulders. Her bare feet shivered against the cold stone floor. She had to act now. Tomorrow would be too late. She had to strike while that minx was out of the castle and her duke was still here. His Grace was an honorable man and he would have to do the right thing. Cecelia may not be his first choice, but she would be his duchess after tonight. In time, he would not even remember he had ever met the Spenser woman. He would only have eyes for his CeCe.

She carefully counted the doors on the hall until she reached his door. She had seen the duke enter the room earlier. She had waited long enough. He should be asleep by now so she could sneak in unnoticed until she wanted to be. She slowly pushed the heavy door open. It creaked. She stopped. No one stirred within. She opened it far enough to let herself in. Then closed the door leaving it slightly ajar. It took a moment for her eyes to adjust to the darkness.

Snores came from the lump in the middle of the bed. She stepped beside the bed and let her robe fall to the floor. She carefully pulled the covers back and slid beneath them. She shivered involuntarily as the cold sheets covered her naked body. The duke was taking up most of the bed. She took a deep breath.

"No. Please. We must not. Please. Stop." Cecelia hollered at the top of her lungs. Then she let out a blood curdling scream. When nothing happened, she hollered again.

Cecelia sobbed louder than ever. "We will have to marry now. You have had your way with me. How could I resist such a powerful man?" She clutched the sheet closer to her naked bosom. Tears wet her cheeks.

Lord Edward whose room was next door rushed toward the scream. He had a burning taper in hand and lit the candle next to the bed. "Lady Cecelia, what has happened? Have you been harmed?"

Cecelia nodded sobbing loudly.

"Madam," a gruff voice spoke from next to her in the bed. "Where exactly do you think you are? More importantly, who do you believe I am?"

The figure in the middle of the bed sat up and pushed his pillow off to the far side of the bed.

"No! No! This is not right. You are supposed to be the duke."

"I am the duke...the Duke of Wingate."

"No! This is all wrong. You are not *my* duke. The young duke. Wallingford. Where is he? What are you doing in his bed?"

Lord Edward stepped a little closer to the bed. "Do you require assistance, Lady Cecelia?"

Cecelia glared and waved him away. He backed toward the door where a crowd was gathering.

"Lady Cecelia. This is my room. I am in my bed. I am afraid you have attempted to entrap the wrong duke. I have not laid a hand on you nor will I be doing so at any point of time in the indefinite future. Get out of my bed! Immediately!" the duke bellowed and pointed to the door.

Cecelia's maid found her way through the throng in the hall and into the room. She retrieved her mistress's robe from the floor. The lady struggled into it, ignored Lord Edward's extended hand, and ran through the crowd of people gathered outside the door. Lord Edward closed the door as he left.

"That woman is totally insane." The duke pulled the pillow off the barely visible smaller form buried under the covers on the side of the bed farthest from the door. "It is all clear now. You may come out, Maggie. Hope I did not smother you."

"I am fine. It was quick thinking to pull the covers over my head and put the pillow there. Thank you for not embarrassing my sons by letting everyone know I was here with you," the Dowager Countess Chelmsford said.

"Darling, I think it is time I made an honest woman of you. How do you feel about becoming the Duchess of Wingate on New Year's Eve?" He leaned over and kissed her cheek.

"I shall let you know in the morning." She winked and snuggled under the covers on her side of the bed.

The duke snuffed out the candle.

****

Grey had slept through Cecelia's entire performance. When he got to breakfast everyone was talking about it.

"I have never understood why she wanted to marry me when I clearly love another?" Grey said to his sister.

"Chalk it up to insanity. I have no other answer," Caroline said. "At least Lady Beatrice found her love match this week. Could two sisters be more different?"

"So is the Duke of Wingate going to marry her since they were caught in a compromising position?"

"No. His Grace made it quite clear to everyone it was all a charade on the part of the lady. She fled his room and packed immediately. Her coach left at first light this morning. Apparently she did not want to be a duchess enough to marry a man old enough to be her grandfather. She only wanted to be *your* duchess, brother dear," Caroline said with a wink.

"And that old duke she tried to entrap belongs to someone else," the Dowager Countess Chelmsford said as she came into the breakfast room on the Duke of

Wingate's arm.

"Mother, would you be that someone?" Paul asked.

"She is indeed," the duke said gleefully. "With the permission of her sons, it is my intention to marry Lady Margaret Winter on New Year's Eve and make her the Duchess of Wingate."

Richard rose and walked to his mother's side. "We would be honored to have you as part of our family, Your Grace." He extended his hand to the duke who shook it enthusiastically.

"I second that sentiment," Paul said.

"Looks like the vicar is going to have a very busy schedule on New Year's Eve," Caroline said.

Chapter Seventeen

Grey pulled the phaeton next to the Harper cottage and parked. The sleigh was fine for a jaunt back to Winterhaven, but he had a longer trip in mind. The partially-covered phaeton would provide some protection from the elements and the two horses a little more speed than the single horse on the sleigh. He straightened his cravat, took a deep breath, and got out. He rapped on the door which was immediately opened by Mrs. Harper.

"Your Grace, we have been expecting you. Welcome to our home." She made a slight curtsey.

He walked in and nodded to Mr. Harper. Emmeline stared at him with her mouth agape. Streaks of red brushed her cheeks. He walked to the table.

"Please sit down and I will fix you a spot of tea, Your Grace," Mrs. Harper said.

"Thank you." Grey searched Emmeline's face for some spark of joy at seeing him. He saw only surprise. "I take it the Harpers did not tell you to expect me this morning."

"Your Grace, we thought it best, given the situation, that you speak for yourself," Harper said.

"I am more than happy to do so if the lady is willing to hear me out."

Emmeline said nothing.

"Your Grace, the missus and I have some chores to

do outside. We will leave you a bit of privacy. C'mon, Mary."

Mrs. Harper set the tea in front of the duke. "We will be right outside, my lady. Do not hesitate to call if you need us, begging your pardon, Your Grace."

Mrs. Harper followed her husband out of the cottage but left the door slightly ajar. Emmeline could see her hovering outside the window.

"Is Cecelia with you?" Emmeline asked.

"No. Of course not. What kind of man brings another woman with him when he has come to ask the love of his life to marry him?"

"You want to marry me? But I saw you kissing her. She said you were eloping to Gretna Green."

"I want to marry you and no one else. I have never kissed Cecelia Thompson or any other woman since I met you. She kissed me but I did not respond positively in any way. I am going to Gretna Green today."

"What?"

"If you say yes, I am going to Gretna Green today. With you. Only with you."

"If I say yes to what?"

Grey got down on one knee and clasped Emmeline's hand in his. "Lady Emmeline Spenser, will you do the honor of becoming my wife and make me the happiest man on earth?"

Tears leaked out of her eyes and splashed down on him. "Yes. Yes. But why Gretna Green? I thought we were going to get married with Eleanor and Simon on New Year's Eve."

"I have found you again and I have no intention of letting you out of my sight until we are legally wed. Not even for five more days. We can be in Gretna Green this evening and return to Winterhaven in time for Eleanor's nuptials. Please, do not make me wait, Emmeline. Say you will elope with me."

"I always thought Ellie and I would get married on the same day. In the same ceremony like our mothers did. We have dreamed about it since we were little girls."

"Please. Trust me. Going to Gretna Green is the best way for us to begin our married life. I promise you will be back in time to celebrate with your cousin."

"I cannot tell you no. Not even if I must give up this lifelong dream. I love you, Grey, and I always will."

She put her arms around his neck. He stood up lifting her off the ground. He put his hands on her waist and twirled her around, then set her on the ground. He tilted her chin up and kissed her slowly and sweetly.

"I love you, Emmeline, and will for the rest of my life. Are you ready for a carriage ride?"

"I cannot yet."

She pulled him down to her and kissed him. Then did it again.

"I believe I have started something. If we want to make Gretna Green tonight, this will have to wait until after the ceremony."

"If you insist, my duke. Oh, I cannot get married in this dress. Mrs. Harper dried it out for me and mended the tear but it is dirty."

"Just a minute. I have a solution."

Grey went outside and moments later returned with a bag.

"Eleanor helped me by packing some things for you."

"So she knew what you planned and approved?"

"Yes. Wholeheartedly."

"I am glad you told Ellie." Emmeline surveyed the room. "There is no where for me to change."

The door creaked open. Mrs. Harper came into the cottage.

"Your Grace, you need to go outside and wait with my mister. You have no business in here while this young lady changes her clothes, begging your pardon. Besides, men are always all thumbs when it comes to buttoning all those tiny nubs up the back. I will let you back in once I have helped the lady into her wedding clothes."

Grey bowed to Emmeline and Mrs. Harper. "I will wait patiently to be readmitted. I would never want to blemish this woman's reputation only hours from the altar." He winked at Emmeline.

Mrs. Harper assisted Emmeline into her gown and brushed her hair. "Yes, my lady, you look like a blushing bride. I am so happy for you." The older woman patted her back.

"Thank you for helping me, Mrs. Harper. I have no idea what I would have done yesterday, if you had turned me away. I am forever grateful." Emmeline leaned over and kissed the woman's wrinkled cheek.

Emmeline stepped out of the cottage and tapped the duke on the shoulder. "I am ready to go, Your Grace." She curtsied.

"You truly are a saucy wench!"

Emmeline was glad for the snug bonnet on her head and warm wool traveling cloak covering her. Grey had a carriage full of robes, furs, and blankets for their journey. She felt toasty warming bricks under her feet.

She snuggled in next to him securely tucked under his arm. He held her close the entire way.

Grey told her about Cecelia's attempt to force him into marriage and the Duke of Wingate and the Dowager Countess Chelmsford's announcement.

"It sounds like there is plenty of marrying to do New Year's Eve without us there," she said.

"Yes, but if you want to have the vicar say a blessing for our marriage, I think it would be nice. Then you would have the second part of your wedding ceremony with Eleanor."

"How sweet of you to suggest this. I am learning more about my almost husband as every mile slides by."

They stopped briefly at midday for a meal at an inn in a small village still in England. Emmeline was too excited to be hungry but she ate since she didn't know when the next opportunity would be.

As darkness began to fall, they reached Gretna Green. Grey stopped the carriage in front of the blacksmith's shop. There were several other buggies and sleighs nearby. The sign said *Marriage Room Within.*

"A blacksmith will conduct our service?" Emmeline asked.

"Yes. They call them anvil priests. That is part of the reason I thought you might appreciate the vicar's blessing on New Year's Eve. The smith can also forge the bride's ring if they would like."

"What an interesting combination of skills— forging marriages and the rings that symbolize them."

"I hope you will not be too disappointed. I have your ring here." Grey withdrew the emerald and diamond wedding band from his pocket.

Emmeline gasped. "What an exquisite ring."

"It was my mother's. My godfather gave it to me the other day with Mother's other fine jewelry."

"I shall treasure it always."

"Shall we go in?"

Grey opened the door. Emmeline let out a shriek and dropped his hand as she entered.

"Ellie. Simon. You are here too. Grey did not tell me you were coming to get married with me!"

"I did not know," Grey confessed.

The cousins hugged and kissed one another's intended.

"Simon knew I was sorry to miss sharing my wedding day with you. It was his suggestion. Being with you on this day is much more important than some elaborate ceremony on New Year's Eve."

"This is perfect. Ellie and Simon can be our witnesses and we can be theirs. Thank you, Simon and Grey. We are two lucky women!"

The fire on the forge was blazing. On the opposite end of the building a small arbor arched over a wooden bench where the Bible lay. Candles were on either side of the Bible. Christmas greenery adorned the bench and arbor.

The smithy walked over to the quartet wiping his hands on a grimy piece of cloth tucked into his belt. He handed Simon a beautiful gold wedding ring.

"Will this do?" Simon showed the ring to Eleanor.

She kissed his cheek. "It is perfect."

The ceremonies were short and sweet. The smithy handed the gentlemen back the licenses after everyone had signed their names. Another couple patiently waited in the doorway for their turn. They did not have any witnesses with them. The smithy's wife and Emmeline signed their license after they were wed.

Then Viscount and Viscountess Summerly and the Duke and Duchess of Wallingford walked across the street to an inn for their shared wedding suppers.

The server came to their table with four mugs of ale. "Compliments of the house. Congratulations."

"How did you know we just married?" Simon asked.

"Look at one another. Have you ever seen bigger smiles on anyone?" The server laughed. She told them the specials and they ordered.

Grey raised his glass. "A toast to our lovely brides. May this be only the first of many celebrations together." They all clinked glasses.

Dinner was simple but filling. Delicious shepherd's pie with creamy brown gravy covering it. For dessert they indulged in delicious apple tarts. They took rooms upstairs in the inn for their first night as man and wife. Simon and Grey made arrangements for their horses while the cousins lingered over a glass of port. When the gentlemen returned they moved upstairs where their rooms were across the hall from one another. The cousins embraced and said "Good night."

Grey unlocked their door and opened it wide for his bride. "Right this way, my duchess."

Blushing, Emmeline stepped into his arms. Grey closed the door. And locked it.

****

Two smiling brides came down to breakfast in the morning on the arms of their grooms. The cousins looked at one another and nodded. Then burst out giggling. Their husbands looked at one another and shrugged.

"We are going to take the long way back to Winterhaven," Simon announced. "I want to stop and introduce my wife to my parents. We will get back to the party by New Year's Eve. We would love to have you and Emmeline come with us."

Emmeline looked at her husband. "Could we, Grey? I would so love to see where Ellie will be living."

"I think it is a splendid idea. But only if Simon and Eleanor agree to come to visit Wallingford in the spring."

Ellie squealed. "How wonderful. I am nervous about meeting Simon's parents. It will be ever so much easier if you are there with me." She clasped her cousin's hand in her own.

"We will lead the way. I expect it will take most of the day to get there. My parents are going to be shocked."

"I hope not because of who you married," Eleanor said defensively.

"No, my love, the fact that I married at all is enough to create a stir. Mother will be delighted with you. I am positive Father will be immediately smitten as I was. Shall we?"

The day began in bright sunshine radiating off the new snow that had fallen overnight. Emmeline and Eleanor enjoyed seeing new scenery. As evening approached the wind increased and it began to snow. Big, fluffy flakes came in the canopy opening of the carriages. Soon the top layer of their cloaks and blankets were glistening white. Simon turned toward a stately manor house on top of a hill.

"Viscountess Summerly, your new home, Summerton."

The exterior of the house shone a pale pink color. A series of steps led to a double door entrance. No sooner had both carriages stopped than the butler came out the door.

"Viscount Summerly, we were not expecting you until the new year. Please come in out of the weather." He helped Eleanor out of the carriage, then Emmeline. They followed him up the steps and into the entrance hall. The butler took their wraps and dispatched one of the houseboys to the stable to tell them to collect the two carriages and horses and get them under shelter.

Eleanor looked around wide-eyed. "Simon, it is simply beautiful and so much larger than I expected."

"Simon!" An elegantly dressed woman with perfectly coiffed silver hair descended the staircase directly in front of them. "Darling, is everything all right? We were not expecting you for at least another five or six days." She walked over and hugged him. "Who have you brought home with you?"

"Mother, everything is better than all right. Please meet my friends, the Duke and Duchess of Wallingford, Greyford and Emmeline Parker, and this wonderful woman is my very special Viscountess Summerly, Eleanor. This is my mother, the Countess of Summerly, Maud Hartsfield."

"Your Graces, I am pleased to welcome you to our home." She stopped in front of Eleanor. "Is it really possible? My son has found a mate? Oh, my dear. You are perfectly lovely." Tears welled up in her eyes. "Eleanor. What a regal name." She extended her arms.

"May I?"

"Of course. Thank you for welcoming me to your beautiful home, Countess," Eleanor said, stepping into her arms.

A distinguished, tall man with silver hair and mustache rounded the corner smoking a pipe. His blue eyes twinkled exactly like Simon's. "Peterson said we have guests who arrived with our prodigal son."

"Indeed you do. Father, I would like you to meet the Duke and Duchess of Wallingford, Greyford and Emmeline Parker. This is my father, the Earl of Summerly, Percy Hartsfield."

"A distinct pleasure, Your Graces."

Maud took Eleanor by the hand and led her to Percy's side. "Darling, I never thought I would be saying these words, but I should like you to meet your daughter-in-law, Eleanor."

"My daughter-in-law? Why you sly devil. How could you keep such a gorgeous woman a secret from your old man?"

"Easily. I only met her a week ago." Simon reddened.

"Just like your mother bowled me over. I am not sure it took a whole week before she had me wedded. These women have mystical powers. You have got to watch them. Say, is your Eleanor a twin?" Percy looked at Emmeline.

"No, sir. They are nearly identical cousins."

Peterson stepped into the hall. "My lady, I have informed Cook we will have four more for dinner."

"Thank you. We need to get you settled in your rooms. Please follow me. I am sure you ladies would like to freshen up a little before dinner. Traveling can be so dirty and tiring." The countess led the way up the broad staircase. "Simon, you and your bride may have your rooms. I will put the duke and duchess in the guest suites. I am certain your bags will be delivered to your rooms shortly. Once you have caught your breath, please join us in the salon. It is a more comfortable place to sit and visit."

An hour later Grey and Emmeline met Simon and Eleanor in the hall. The viscount led the way to the salon where his parents were waiting. The countess patted the sofa cushion next to her.

"Eleanor, my dear, please sit close to me. I want to know all about your whirlwind courtship. I can hardly believe I am finally a mother-in-law."

"My cousin and the duke are newlyweds too. We have all just come from Gretna Green."

"Then we have lots to talk about. Tell me everything."

Chapter Eighteen

During the course of the evening the quartet told Simon's parents all about the week-long courtship including the original identity swap.

"Are you certain you married the right one?" Simon's father asked with a wink.

"Oh, yes. I know the secret of how to tell them apart now." Simon winked back.

"Yours did not have a dowry?" his father asked.

"That is the delicious irony. We both thought that was true but it turns out Eleanor did."

"What will your parents think of the elopement?" Maud asked.

"My parents are gone. Emmeline's father, Lord Crestmont, is my guardian." Eleanor said.

"I asked for Eleanor's hand the day after Christmas and the duke asked for Emmeline's at the same time. Later Wallingford told the earl he was not waiting until New Year's Eve for a wedding but eloping. I believe the earl's response was 'good for you.' We decided it was a good idea as well," Simon explained.

"It is my fault we did not wait for an official ceremony. I could not bear the thought of Emmeline marrying without me being there with her," Eleanor said softly.

"I am glad you did. I got to meet you a week sooner than I would have," Maud said.

"Oh, Mother, William is getting married on New Year's Eve to a lovely woman, Lady Beatrice Thompson. They are going to wed at Winterhaven."

"Are they a good match?"

"Yes. Almost as well-suited as Eleanor is to me."

"It sounds like the countess's holiday house party is going to be a raging success. Lots of new families starting out," Maud said.

"We are planning to ask the vicar to bless our marriages during the other wedding services New Year's Eve. Perhaps you would like to come back to Winterhaven with us to be there for the ceremony," Grey suggested.

"I hate to impose on the countess but I would love to be there. After all, your only son marries just once," Maud said. "What do you think, Percy?"

"Why not? When will you be returning to the castle?"

"I thought we would leave in the morning," Simon responded.

"Why not stay one more day and show your new bride and her cousin around the estate?" his mother said. "I think she might be especially interested in Spring Hill."

"What is Spring Hill?" Eleanor asked.

"It is the dower house," Maud responded.

"Dower house? You mean we will not be living here with you?" Eleanor asked.

"You are certainly welcome to live here if you want. I thought as newlyweds you might like the privacy of a home of your own. Spring Hill has been empty for four years. It would need some sprucing up but it is quite lovely. I have very fond memories of living there as a new bride." Maud's cheeks reddened as she met her husband's eyes.

"Are you shocked your mother has everything ready for your surprise new bride? She has been planning for this day ever since you turned twenty. I will not tell you how many baby booties she has knitted over the last two years waiting for you to marry and produce grandchildren," Percy said.

Eleanor blushed bright red. "You are very kind to offer us a home of our own. Simon, I would love to see it if we can delay our return to Winterhaven long enough."

"Tomorrow is only the 29th. We can leave the morning of the 30th and be back in plenty of time for the New Year's Eve activities. Do you agree, Wallingford?"

"Yes. And my sister will be more than happy to have you join the party for the nuptials," Grey said.

"Your sister?"

"Yes. The Countess Chelmsford is my twin."

"Will she have enough room for two more?" Maud asked.

"You could take the room Eleanor and I have been sharing since we can move in with our husbands."

"Excellent idea, my sweet wife. It is settled. We will accept your gracious hospitality here at Summerton for one more day and travel day after tomorrow."

After breakfast, Simon suggested they go for a ride around the property. The stablemaster brought one of the sleighs to the front of Summerton. It was pulled by a perfectly matched pair of pale gray horses. Simon and Eleanor got into the front seat and Grey and Emmeline behind them.

The estate was bordered by a small river on two sides and vast woods between the manor house and the charming village. The village boasted a blacksmith shop, a tinsmith, a leather worker, and a pub. A sawmill was on the edge of the river. There were a few wagons selling freshly slaughtered meat and winter vegetables. Thirty families lived on the estate working the farm land and harvesting the timber. A number of the stable and manor workers lived there with their families as well.

People recognized the Viscount Summerly as they traveled through the area. He proudly introduced his new bride and her cousin and spouse to everyone they met. Snow-covered fields lay beyond the village. Simon cut across them to the other side of Summerton. There on a small rise overlooking the partially frozen river was Spring Hill.

The two-story white stone structure seemed at least three-quarters as large as Summerton. Ornamental hedges lined the cobblestone drive in front of the house. A small fountain topped with Cupid's statue was beyond the hedges circled by stone benches.

They stopped the sleigh in front of the dower house. The door opened and a young woman in a maid's uniform came out.

"Viscount and Viscountess Summerly, welcome to your new home," she said with a curtsey.

"Good morning. I did not know anyone was here."

"My lord, the countess asked me to come over and begin cleaning. My name is Mary. My mother is the cook at Summerton. I hope to be your cook and maid here, if I will meet your needs."

Eleanor stepped forward and took the young

woman's hand. "I am certain you will be perfect for the job. Thank you coming over early to welcome us."

"Proud to do it, my lady. Please come in." Mary led the way up three steps and into the entrance hall.

"I have not been here since Grandmama died but I can give you a short tour. We will begin upstairs. Mary, feel free to return to your work." Simon led the way up the steps.

Upstairs held five bedrooms including the master suite with a sitting room, bedroom, and bath. There were three large bathrooms, each with a deep claw-foot tub. The furniture was covered with dust cloths. Eleanor and Emmeline peeked under some of them to find richly upholstered, heavy dark wood furniture. The draperies were heavy damask and in good condition. The color scheme was calming. Everything was a bit musty smelling but nothing a little airing out could not solve.

Downstairs there was a formal living room, a library, a smaller salon where Simon remembered his grandmother serving tea, a dining room large enough to seat sixteen, a solarium, a small breakfast room, and a huge kitchen. Each of the rooms had elegant appointments. The living room and salon had massive stone fireplaces. Beyond the kitchen were quarters for four staff members. Ornamental gardens with a hedge maze and cobblestone path were behind the house. At the back of the property was a small greenhouse.

Simon embraced his wife. "Well, darling, will it do?"

"Surely you jest. It is beyond my wildest expectations for my first married home. I am overwhelmed. It is positively perfect."

"You will be so happy here, Ellie. It is lovely. And plenty of room for visitors and children," Emmeline said.

"Mother will be glad you like it. I think it made her a little sad when she had to move up to Summerton. My parents seemed very happy here. We should probably go back to the house for luncheon. I am certain Mother is on pins and needles waiting to hear the verdict."

Maud greeted them at the door. She hugged Eleanor. "What did you think?"

"Countess, it is exquisite. Thank you for offering such a lovely home to us."

"Eleanor, I am your mother-in-law. We need not be so formal. Please do not call me Countess."

"What would you prefer? Lady Summerly?"

"No. You could call me Maud…or even Mother, like Simon does, if you were comfortable with that."

Tears welled up in both women's eyes. Eleanor said, "I would be honored to call you Mother. Thank you for making my transition to new wife so perfect. I do not know what more I could ask for."

****

The next morning's sky was full of sunshine and blue skies as a trio of carriages began their trek to Winterhaven. Light snow covered the path the entire way but the air wasn't too cold to enjoy the journey. They stopped at a small inn a little past midday for a bite to eat and to stretch their legs. As the sun almost reached the Pennine mountain tops, they crossed the drawbridge into the bailey in front of Winterhaven castle.

Two young boys raced out of the keep to meet them before they had a chance to disembark.

"Uncle Grey, we missed you." Stephen said.

"Did you go on an adventure without us?" Oliver asked.

"You might say that," Grey said as he tousled their hair. "Let us get out of the cold and into the keep. We shall tell you all about it before dinner."

The trio of carriages unloaded. As Grey predicted, Lady Chelmsford was more than happy to welcome Lord and Lady Summerly. Emmeline was correct. They would take the cousins' room. Their things had been moved in with their husbands.

They gathered in the gold salon to visit before dinner. Caroline called her sons to her side.

"Oliver and Stephen, while Uncle Grey was gone on the adventure he got married," she announced. "That means you have an aunt now."

"What is that?" Oliver asked.

"When one of your uncles gets married his wife becomes your aunt. Lady Emmeline married Uncle Grey so she is related to you now. She is your aunt."

"Mother, do you mean Miss Brown?" Stephen corrected her.

"No, she was really Lady Emmeline. Remember? She was just making believe she was Miss Brown. Now she is the Duchess of Wallingford."

"So does that make her Aunt Grey?" Oliver asked.

"Why not ask her what she would like to be called?"

The boys stood in front of Grey and Emmeline.

"Your Grace, what should we call you?" Stephen asked.

"What about Aunt Emmie? Would that work?" Emmeline asked.

"Uncle Grey and Aunt Emmie. I like it," Stephen said.

"So Mother, when do we get more aunts?" Oliver asked.

"Not until Uncle Paul gets married. Your Papa only has one brother, Paul. And I only have one brother, Grey. You have two uncles and some day you will have two aunts."

Paul said, "You shall have two aunts tomorrow evening after the weddings."

Caroline gasped. "Who? You have not said a word."

Paul walked to the chair Cornelia was sitting in. "Lord Bollingwood gave me his consent and Cornelia said 'yes' only this afternoon. We plan to join the others and be wed tomorrow evening."

The Dowager Countess hugged her younger son. "Cornelia was a precious little girl who has grown into a lovely young woman. I could not be happier. Do you think this will be a first for a mother and son to both be wed in the same ceremony?"

"I had not thought of that, Mother. It may be. Are you moving to the duke's home after you wed?" Paul asked.

"I will answer that," the Duke of Wingate said. "Absolutely. Why else would I be marrying her?"

The dowager countess clapped her hands. "Yes, Paul. I know what you are thinking. It would be perfect for the two of you. Cornelia will love living in the dower house. Then I can come one place to visit both of you and your families."

"Whose aunt is Miss Eleanor now?" Oliver asked soberly.

"Miss Eleanor is now Lady Summerly," his mother corrected him.

Eleanor knelt beside the boy. "I am afraid no one's. I have no brothers or sisters and Lord Summerly does not either. So I have no little boys to be an aunt to."

"But Aunt Emmie should count. She is almost your sister, is she not?" Oliver asked.

"Mother, could Aunt Emmie and Aunt Cornelia share us with Lord and Lady Summerly? Otherwise they will be so sad. Everyone should get to be an aunt and uncle," Stephen said.

Caroline said, "What do you think, Emmeline and Cornelia?"

The women looked at one another and nodded. They joined Eleanor kneeling beside the boys.

"I cannot think of anyone else I would rather share you with than my sweet cousin and her husband," Emmeline said.

"I agree. The boys should have at least three aunts and uncles," Cornelia said.

"Hooray!" Oliver said.

The boys hugged their new aunties and then their mother before fleeing the room to the nursery.

The butler came into the room and went to Lord Castleberry's side. He handed him a piece of paper. "My lord, the messenger is in the hallway. Should he wait for a response?"

He quickly read the note and followed the butler to the hall. Moments later, Lord Castleberry asked for Lord Glenwood to join him in the entrance hall.

When they returned to the salon, Lord Castleberry announced, "The messenger was from my son, Edward, who left the day after Christmas to attend to some family business in Scotland. He met Lady Cecelia on the road and the two of them wed at Gretna Green on the 27th. They will return home after the new year."

After a moment for the surprising news to register, Lady Beatrice said, "I am so glad my sister was able to find her mate. I hope they will be very happy."

"Dinner is served," the butler said.

Grey offered his arm to his wife and stopped at his sister's side. "I think, Caro, your matchmaking has been highly successful. When the new year rolls in, you will not have a solitary unmarried person over the age of eighteen within the walls of this castle."

"You are correct. Although I must confess the pairings did not work quite the way I expected. Are you glad you came?" she teased her twin.

"I do not know about him, but I am delighted he did!" Emmeline said.

Epilogue

New Year's Eve mid-morning it began to snow.
Hard. Throughout the day worried couples looked out
on the glistening powder accumulating on the bailey.
Lady Chelmsford enlisted everyone to help with
redecorating the Great Hall in preparation for the
wedding ceremonies. At least, if their hands were busy
maybe they would stop worrying about when the vicar
would arrive. She continued to send up fervent prayers
for the holy man to appear. All her matchmaking would
be for naught if no one came to tie the nuptial knots.

The ceremonies were planned for between tea time
and dinner. A buffet feast was being prepared for that
night's celebrations.

Luncheon consisted of hearty bread and soup.
Nothing more was needed because many of the guests
were too nervous to eat.

Oliver and Stephen coaxed Uncle Grey and Aunt
Emmie out onto the bailey to build another snowman.
Yes, there was that much snow. At tea time they were
all apple red cheeked and shivering. Lady Chelmsford
had cocoa waiting for the boys and extra hot tea for her
brother and sister-in-law.

Only an hour before the ceremonies were
scheduled to begin Vicar Bronson arrived at
Winterhaven with his wife, Leora. He was greeted by a
greatly relieved hostess and five very happy couples.

Lady Chelmsford ordered some tea to warm them up and showed them to their room. Shortly later the vicar and his wife walked into the Great Hall which had been transformed into a wedding setting.

Tables were set up along one wall for the wedding feast to be arrayed on. The fireplaces were roaring, creating a warm and welcoming atmosphere in the room. On the opposite wall from the buffet table, an arbor had been created by weaving together evergreen boughs extracted from the Christmas tree and interspersing holly and mistletoe throughout them. In front of the arbor a bench with two candles and a cross created an altar. Benches were lined up on both sides of an aisle and there was plenty of space in front of the pews for the five couples—two for blessings and three for a complete ceremony.

The guests filtered in a few at a time. When everyone was seated, the vicar walked down the center aisle and took his place behind the altar. He began by announcing the names of the couples being married and asking if anyone knew of any reason why they could not be. After waiting what seemed like an excessive amount of time, no objections were made and the ceremonies continued.

Lady Beatrice Thompson and William Benedict, Viscount Ashleigh, walked hand-in-hand down the aisle. They said their vows and stepped to the left of the main aisle. The Honorable Paul Winter and Lady Cornelia Peters came down the aisle holding hands. With the vicar's guidance they said their vows and stepped to the right. The Duke of Wingate, Jonathon Marley, and the Dowager Countess of Chelmsford, Margaret Winter, linked arms and walked down the aisle. After saying their vows, they stayed where they were.

The Duke and Duchess of Wallingford, Greyford and Emmeline Parker, walked down the aisle together followed by the Viscount and Viscountess Summerly, Simon and Eleanor Hartsfield. The two couples stood immediately behind the three just-married pairs. The vicar bowed his head and raised his arms. He prayed the official wedding blessing asking for lifelong love and fruitfulness for the couples before him.

The guests stood and applauded when the prayer ended. There were hugs and kisses all around.

The kitchen staff began bringing out the feast. The hunting expedition had provided hearty roast venison, tender swans stuffed with clams, juicy pheasant surrounded by boiled leeks and potatoes, a thick and aromatic rabbit stew served with hunks of fresh-baked oaten bread, and roasted geese on platters surrounded by onions and carrots.

Lord Chelmsford had his best wines from his private cellars opened and generously shared them with his guests. Tankards of ale and mead were available to all who wanted it.

Stephen went over to the new Duchess of Wingate and tugged on her sleeve, "Grandmama, will you still be our grandmama even after you go away with the duke?"

She bent down and kissed the top of his head. "Of course, my darling. But now you have a grandpapa as well. Is that not wonderful?"

"Hooray! Oliver we have three new aunties, a new uncle, and even a grandpapa!" Stephen shouted to his brother.

"We are such lucky boys! Are we not, Mother?" Oliver shouted.

"Indeed you are. You are the luckiest boys I know," their mother said.

What a wonderful way to end one year! And a marvelous start for the next!

A word about the author...

I grew up in a small town in Wisconsin. I had a career in Healthcare Information Technology, most recently as CIO for a small hospital group in Alabama. Now, I am focused on creative endeavors - writing, spinning, weaving, knitting, crocheting, and creating buildings for my husband's model railroad. I have been married to my own Romance hero for almost forever.

Follow my adventures at www.spinningromance.com.
E-mail me at kimjanine@spinningromance.com. I'd love to hear from my readers!

Printed in the USA
CPSIA information can be obtained
at www.ICGtesting.com
LVHW021409041224
798129LV00003B/515